THE GLASS CASE

Recent Titles by Anne Goring from Severn House

BITTER HARVEST
KATE WEATHERBY
NO ENEMY BUT WINTER

THE GLASS CASE

Anne Goring

This first world edition published in Great Britain 1999 by
SEVERN HOUSE PUBLISHERS LTD of
9–15 High Street, Sutton, Surrey SM1 1DF.
This title first published in the U.S.A. 1999 by
SEVERN HOUSE PUBLISHERS INC of
595 Madison Avenue, New York, N.Y. 10022.

British Library Cataloguing in Publication Data

Goring, Anne
    The glass case
    I.   Title
    823.9'14 [F]

    ISBN 0 7278 5412 7

Typeset by Palimpsest Book Production Ltd
Polmont, Stirlingshire, Scotland
Printed and bound in Great Britain by
MPG Books Ltd, Bodmin, Cornwall.

One

The sun was hot, very hot, and there was a pervasive, insistent stench wafting into the air.

Polly Burton stalked round the half-buried carcass of the tiger shark, the shrewdly professional part of her mind assessing the shape of the shark against the sand, the cloud of attendant flies and the backcloth of breaking rollers creaming in huge smooth swoops up to the tideline. Automatically, she noted the angle of the sun striking down from the hard blue sky and the contrast between the picture postcard background and the gruesome relic in the foreground. Worth a couple of shots, she decided.

She crouched to focus the Canon. The camera clicked and clicked again. She moved to a different viewpoint but instantly regretted it. She was directly downwind and the smell was overpowering. Hastily she stood up and backed off. The queasy feeling she'd been trying to ignore as she'd trekked across the curve of white beach in the late-morning heat intensified. Despite the shady straw hat she wore, the sun seemed to be boring a hole in her head.

It had been a mistake to walk so far in her fragile state, even though she had believed that she'd fully recovered from the stomach upset which had bothered her for a couple of days.

1

Both Polly and her aunt had been smitten just after they arrived in Durban. Aunt Hester had planned that they should spend the last few days of their holiday relaxing in the hedonistic splendour of a luxury hotel on the coast of Natal. After nearly three weeks of safaris in various game parks it was ironic that they had scarcely a mosquito bite to show for the nights spent in the bush or in remote lodges, yet they had succumbed the moment they hit civilisation. But the pills Aunt Hester had produced from her well-stocked medicine kit and the attention they had received from the solicitous hotel staff had worked wonders.

"One must expect these little discomforts from time to time when one wishes to see the world," Aunt Hester had said airily this morning as she sat swathed in her favourite silk kimono, managing to look as glamorous as ever despite two miserable days. "And if one must be ill, where better than a place like this?" She waved at the cream and gold room, at the tall windows framing the balcony and the view of the Indian Ocean beyond. She frowned at Polly. "Do you really propose to go yomping off because the chambermaid told you some disgusting dead thing has been washed up on the beach? Goodness me, haven't you got enough snaps for one holiday?"

"Those 'snaps' are my bread and butter," Polly said, mildly.

"But this was supposed to be a proper holiday for you," her aunt declared with a pretence at being peeved, for she knew perfectly well that Polly's devotion to her craft all too often blurred the boundaries between work and leisure. "Not some extended work project."

"It's been wonderful." Polly bent to give her aunt a

hug. "I wouldn't have missed a minute of it. Especially the game parks. So I forgive you, Aunt Hes, for nagging my socks down until I submitted to your evil scheme to drag me to Africa."

"So you should!" Aunt Hester's green eyes sparked with pleasure, despite her tart words. For all her teasing banter, she was deeply fond and very proud of this niece of hers. "And as I'm in a particularly amiable mood this morning, I'll say no more about the hideous delays I've suffered these last weeks while you've been waiting for the light to fall precisely on a certain twig or for some wild beast to arrange itself photogenically."

Polly grinned. "When you see the pictures you'll know why. And you were an angel of patience while I was being so tiresome. I'm eternally grateful."

"But a dead shark, darling." Aunt Hester gave a fastidious shudder. "Surely that's a pleasure you could easily forgo?"

Polly was beginning to think so too as she stepped away from the noisome creature. She really was starting to feel quite ill again. Her legs seemed likely give way any second and her stomach was seriously revolted by the smell of decay.

She narrowed her eyes against the light, staring back across the empty stretch of dazzling sand. She'd walked much further than she'd realised. The hotel seemed of doll's house proportions. Or perhaps it was a trick of her suddenly uncertain vision.

She knew that it was imperative to get out of the sun for a few minutes, to rest in the shade and recover enough to contemplate making the return journey. But she saw with dismay that there was little shelter at this end of the beach. She'd left the last clump of picturesquely leaning palms some way behind, and the fringe of low thorny bushes above the beach looked singularly inhospitable. But beyond the bushes was the service road that led to the hotel. Maybe if her head would stop its sickening spinning she could get that far and hope for a lift back. She thought ruefully of the quiet opulence of her room. Although she hadn't exactly been enamoured with the idea of spending these precious last days in the sort of hotel that could be found anywhere in the world and where, for the benefit of its international clientele, the vast complexities of Africa were reduced to sanitised displays of tribal dancing and tasteful artifacts on sale in the arcade of expensive boutiques, the comfort of her king-sized bed and the purring chill of air-conditioning now seemed infinitely desirable.

She put the camera back into its protective padded case, looped it over her shoulder and forced her uncertain legs to move.

Heat reflected from the sand in shimmering waves as she began to struggle up the slope of the beach. The surf boomed in her ears. Every step seemed a tremendous effort and despite the heat she felt the shivery, sickly onset of faintness. She found it hard to focus her eyes. Oh, hell! She couldn't pass out here. She had to find some sort of shelter.

A few more staggering steps and she reached a bush. She scarcely felt the scratch of thorns against her bare legs as she lurched past, arms outstretched like a blind person. Then, suddenly, there was a shadow in front of her. She sensed rather than saw it. She was being drawn too fast into the darkness to care who it was she stumbled into, scarcely heard the deep voice, saying in surprise,

4

"Good grief, that's my shirt you're attacking, madam." Then, in a different tone of voice altogether. "I've got you. Here . . ."

"Need . . . need . . . sorry . . ." She couldn't form words.

Her knees sagged. The darkness possessed her.

Consciousness returned slowly. She became aware that she was sitting down and that she was scrunched over, her head on her knees. Warily she opened her eyes, focusing first on a scrap of sun-bleached canvas under her thighs – she was sitting on some sort of camp chair – then on her feet. Need a new pair of trainers, she noted absently. Pity. They were so comfortable, battered though they might be. Around her feet, blades of coarse grass thrust up through the sand. Several rust-coloured ants were negotiating the lumpy terrain around her right foot. Huge ants. Different. Like the broad-bladed grass. The heat. She wasn't at home. Of course not, but where . . . ?

Recollection flooded back and she tried to sit up, but she couldn't move. Something was holding her head down.

"Stay where you are for a minute longer." A voice, vaguely remembered. A man's voice. The next instant something sloshed against her skin, shocking her into a squeak of protest.

"Ice cubes," said the man gruffly, holding them against the nape of her neck. "Should do the trick."

Polly shuddered. Trickles of water slid down her spine and round her neck to drip onto the crumpled navy cotton of her shorts.

"Feeling better?"

"Y . . . yes. I think so," she said in a muffled voice.

"Take a few deep breaths. Don't sit up suddenly."

Gingerly she straightened. The world reeled for a few seconds before settling. The sick feeling in her stomach eased and, with a rush of embarrassment, she realised that she had made a complete fool of herself. Oh, God, fancy falling into a swoon like a Victorian maiden!

Her rescuer, whoever he was, had moved to one side. She heard the fizzing noise of a bottle being opened and the sound of liquid being poured. Then the man was standing over her, a dark bulky shape against the sun, holding out a plastic cup.

"I've put the last ice cube in," he said. "Take your time. Sip it slowly. It's only fizzy mineral water."

"Th . . . thanks," she said. Her hand shook as she took the cup. "You're very kind."

"Glad to help. If you'd like coffee, there's some left in the flask."

"No, no. This is fine."

She was sitting under a golf umbrella which was tied with a length of rope to a walking stick stuck into the sand. On a khaki-coloured groundsheet was a scatter of equipment: a pair of binoculars, a camera, several notebooks and pens, and a blue coolbag open to reveal bottles of Evian water and a couple of large thermos flasks. Someone was well prepared against heat and dehydration.

"Feeling better?"

"Much. I'll . . . I'll get out of your way in a minute."

"Oh, yes?" She caught an edge of dry amusement. "You're from that hotel at the other end of the beach?"

She nodded. It wasn't a wise thing to do. She closed her eyes again. Her brain felt like flannel.

"That's a fair distance."

"So I discovered," she said wishing her voice didn't sound so feeble.

"Well, you're in no state to walk back," he said. "Give me a few minutes to clear this lot away and I'll give you a lift. My car's parked back there."

"Oh, I couldn't put you to such—"

"It's no trouble." An English voice. Deep, quiet and authoritative. She couldn't find the energy to argue. She just wanted to sit here, eyes closed and let him get on with what he had to do. "I'm just about finished here anyway."

She listened to him moving about. She'd be okay in a minute or two. He sounded respectable enough. But you never knew. She could think properly about it if her head would stop its sickly spinning . . .

"So what brought you trekking down the beach?" he asked. There was a flapping noise as he shook sand from the rug.

"A tiger shark. Washed up by the tide. I wanted to photograph it."

"That thing? Not much left to photograph is there?" Again that edge of dry amusement. "And stinking to high heaven."

"So I found out." She screwed her eyes half open against the dazzle and took a sip of the water. "My . . . my camera?"

"Safe in the car. Where you'll be in a minute. Just have to take down the umbrella . . . There. Sorry, I'll have to leave you in the sun while I throw this in the boot. Won't be a tick."

The heat hit her as he took down the umbrella but he was back quickly, a firm hand under her arm, helping her up, managing to fold up the camp chair with his

7

free hand, urging her forward. "Take it easy now. It's not far."

Her legs felt like chewed string as they moved through the scrub, sand scuffing into little clouds around their feet. She could do nothing other than lean on him and hope she made the car without throwing up.

"I've never done anything like this in my life before," she said weakly. "Faint, I mean. It's just that I've been ill for a couple of days. What with that and the heat . . ."

"All a bit too much, eh? Here's the car. Can you manage?"

She subsided thankfully onto the passenger seat, even though the heat inside seemed more stifling than outside. He fastened the seat belt round her.

"My camera?" she said again, clinging to the one certainty in an insubstantial, wavering world.

He reached it from the back seat and placed it carefully on her lap. She felt the roughness of the case under her fingers.

"Keen photographer are you?"

"Professional."

"Really?"

He closed the door, ran round to the driver's seat. "Hang in there," he said, starting up the engine. "Have you back in a jiffy. What kind of work?"

"What?"

"Your photography."

"Freelance."

"Photo-journalism?"

"No. Architectural mostly. Some ad agency stuff."

"So decaying sharks make quite a change. You're here in a professional capacity, then?"

"Holiday. With my aunt."

Every bump in the road threatened disaster.

"Take deep breaths," he ordered. "Concentrate on what I'm saying and try to keep your eyes open. Come on, now. Open your eyes. You're not going to faint again. Only a few more minutes and we're there. You've been to the game parks?"

She made an enormous effort.

"Serengeti. Kruger . . ." She took one slow, deep breath after another, forced her lids open.

"Great stuff. Once you've been to places like that you're hooked for life. At least that's my experience. Good girl, that's it. Mind over matter. I'm a great believer in it. See, we're running alongside the hotel grounds now."

A blur of colour among the greenery. The hotel buildings, sugar-pink rising from great swathes of scarlet, hot purple and carmine bougainvillea; beds of geraniums, canna lilies, oleanders . . . the shimmering turquoise curves of the swimming pool.

She wasn't going to be sick. She wasn't going to faint. She was beating down the feeling of nausea, thank heaven. Another steadying breath and she carefully turned her head to look at this man, her rescuer. She had the words ready to thank him, but they suddenly choked in her throat.

She'd had the impression of height, of a solid muscular body. Someone who was comfortable to lean on. Middle aged, probably, very concerned and kind, almost paternal. But she saw he was nothing like that. Nothing at all.

It was a harsh, almost fierce, profile.

Jutting curving nose, strong black brows frowning in concentration, black curling hair, down-curved mouth. A face of harsh, bony angles and a jaw covered with swarthy

9

stubble. Not a kindly face, nor a fatherly one. The face of a buccaneer, a bandit.

Danger!

Panic hit her like a fist slamming into her solar plexus, choked every thought except the need for flight. She must get away! She must get out of this car. Away from *him*. Away from danger. Her fingers grabbed at the door handle.

"I found myself with a couple of spare hours on my way to Durban for a meeting." His voice, relaxed and easy, smoothed gently through the panic. "Thought I'd make the most of it. Find a quiet spot and indulge in some bird watching. Lucky for you I did, or heaven knows how long you'd have been stuck out in the sticks. I only saw a couple of locals legging it down the road and not many cars all the time I was there. Ah, here we are. That wasn't too bad, was it? You'll soon be safely tucked up in your hotel room."

The car slowed, turned between the tall gateposts. She saw the familiar face of the gatekeeper. The car proceeded slowly along the drive.

Oh, God, she'd nearly blown it. Whatever would he have thought if she'd flung herself out of the car? This kind man who meant no harm, who had rescued her. Must have been the faint, the illness. It was so long since anything like that had happened.

She hastily removed her hand from the door and slid it back on to her lap, though her heart still thumped under her ribs so loud she thought he might hear it. And, as though he had, he took his attention from the road and glanced at her.

The turn of his head brought subtle change, banishing the harshness of his profile. Blue eyes, clear and shrewd, regarded her with amiable concern from beneath black brows that had lost their ferocious frown.

"Well done," he said.

For a confusing moment she thought he was congratulating her for not bursting open the door and leaping out of the car in a blind panic. Then, common sense reasserted itself. He was merely pleased that she was still conscious and hadn't wilted – or worse – all over him and his car.

The rush of panic-driven adrenalin through her system had certainly banished that possibility. She was alert enough now, too alert. All her senses seemed ultra-sharp under the influence of the primitive instinct for self-preservation that had overpowered her. Involuntarily, a scene she'd witnessed a few days ago in Kruger sprang into her head.

There had been a small herd of springbok grazing peacefully by a waterhole, but something had spooked them and the whole herd had leapt away in seconds and vanished into the bush. She had caught it on camera. A moment of pure grace and beauty, as fear powered them into leaping, dancing flight. Now she recognised in herself that need, that urgency to flee the predator.

So much for the millennia of human development, she thought dryly, that a moment of weakness – and it *was* only the wretched result of the illness – could reduce even the most sensible of women to the level of a terror-stricken prey animal. Thank God there had been no one to witness that moment of terror. And it must have showed. It had enveloped her too suddenly, too overpoweringly, for her to mask her expression or body language. But she had overcome it, and this stranger was surely too busy with his driving to have noticed. If it had been Aunt Hester or Charles it would have been a different matter. They

11

knew her too well not to have been concerned. And the last thing she would have wanted was to suffer well-meant questions. Nor would she have wished to upset them in any way, those two dearest and closest people in her life.

Charles. The still-shaking fingers of her right hand reached for the third finger of her left and gripped the square-cut solitaire diamond. She took comfort from the familiar feel of it. Soon she would be back home. Back with Charles and her well-ordered, comfortable routine. Think of that. Don't think of the past, of the bad things.

The car pulled in under the deep shade of the entrance porch. She fumbled again with the door handle as her rescuer cut the engine.

"You've been very kind," she began, "but I mustn't trouble you any further."

"No trouble." He was already out of the car and moving round to the passenger side.

"I'm quite recovered. Really," she protested.

She wasn't and she knew it. The phobic, sweating moment of panic still surged in her subconscious. Her heart still beat a tattoo under her ribs. Her legs still wobbled uncertainly as, with his hand firmly under her elbow, they went the few steps into the blissful air-conditioned chill of the high-ceilinged, marble-floored foyer.

He steered her towards a deep sofa.

"If you sit here I'll get help. Is your aunt in the hotel at present? Shall I have her paged? I could see you to your room, but perhaps you'd prefer one of the maids—"

"Look, I'll be okay now," she said. Her voice was firmer. She was beginning to take control of the panic; facing it as she had painfully taught herself to do over the years, forcing herself to assess the reasons why it had happened. It was the physical after-effects of her illness, of course. Her defences had been eroded by the tide of faintness, her vulnerability heightened by the stranger's insistence on taking charge. None of this was his fault, and he had acted with impeccable competence and concern. He couldn't help his looks.

His hand was still on her arm. Polly moved, shrugging away his touch but smiling politely because she didn't wish to hurt his feelings.

"Thanks, but there's no need to bother anyone else. And I've wasted enough of your time."

"You still look pretty white and shaky to me. Let me at least see you to Reception. Now we've got this far I wouldn't want you collapsing in a heap on the home stretch."

"I won't," she said, wishing all the same that the lift wasn't at the far side of the foyer. Wishing, too, that he wouldn't stand there – large, solid, immovable. Threatening. No, no, no! It wasn't like that at all. She mustn't give way to feverish imaginings. "I don't need to go to Reception. I have my room key in my pocket. One of those card things. I just need to get to the lift."

"To the lift then."

Thankfully, he made no attempt to take her arm, though he walked close enough to catch her if she did stumble. An elderly lady waiting there had already pressed the bell and the lift was on its way down.

Polly turned to her rescuer and held out her hand.

"Thanks again," she said.

"Glad to be of help," he said. The indentations at the corners of his mouth deepened as he smiled, though the sharp blue eyes regarded her gravely and she thought for a stupid moment that he might insist on accompanying her upstairs. But his hand folded around her own, the palm warm and slightly rough. "Take care."

"I will." Then she added somewhat awkwardly, realising that she should at least attempt to be more gracious, "I . . . I don't know what I'd have done if you hadn't been there. I'm truly very grateful."

"My pleasure," he said. "Hope you're soon feeling better."

"I'm sure I shall be."

She pulled her hand away and followed the elderly lady into the lift, making a business of selecting the right floor button so that she wouldn't have to look at him again. But as the lift doors drew together her gaze was drawn to the narrowing gap. He'd stepped back but was still watching her. He lifted his hand in farewell. A tall, black-haired bandit with smiling eyes.

Then the doors closed and he was gone.

Leon Hammond's smile disappeared abruptly as the lift doors closed. He frowned as he stared at the panel where the illuminated floor numbers clicked over. Then, with a half shrug he turned away and walked slowly, lost in thought, across to the main door. But, almost there, he stopped, hesitated, and turned back towards the reception desk.

The sharply elegant, middle-aged woman who supervised Reception watched him. Her mouth tightened. She had noted the little scene played out in the foyer as she noted everything that went on in the little realm she ruled with glacial efficiency, and she regarded the man's approach with a decided touch of frost. The standard of the clientele these days! She cast a nostalgic thought back to her youth when everyone conformed to the smart casual dress demanded of a hotel of this calibre. Once upon a time no one would have dared to walk in here in ragged cut-off jeans and a shabby T-shirt. And if they had, they would have had the decency to be overawed and uneasy, rather than stride in with an air of calm unconcern.

She edged the junior duty clerk out of the way. "I'll deal with this," she said, running her red-taloned hand down the smooth tailoring of her cream and pink uniform jacket as though searching for a recalcitrant crease.

Her loyalty to the hotel, its profitability and its reputation for superb service, vied with her personal inclination to send this species of sweaty beach bum packing with a flea in his ear. But she was unexpectedly taken aback when he leant a confident elbow on the counter and looked her in the eye. Despite his unshaven state, rumpled hair and disgraceful attire, she recognised him.

She did a quick reassessment, setting that suddenly familiar face in a different context. A sycophantic interest swept away the frigidity of her stare. Nothing would change her opinion on today's dress code but she knew better than to upset anyone of such potential value to the hotel. Besides with his line of work, she might reasonably allow herself a little leeway in her evaluation of his clothing. His was hardly the kind of profession that demanded a suit and tie, now, was it? Perhaps he had walked in here direct from some assignment.

"May I help you, sir?" she enquired, in her most genteel and deferential tone so that the junior clerk looked up to see who the old bat was soft-soaping now. He grinned to himself when he saw who it was. Only the presence of the rich and famous ever produced that particular level of obsequiousness.

"The young lady I just came in with. I'd like to send her some flowers."

"Miss Burton, sir?" Well, well. Such a dowdy uninteresting girl, too. "Certainly, sir. We have a florist in the mall if you—"

"No time, unfortunately." He glanced at his watch. "I hadn't realised it had got so late and I've a meeting in Durban. Could you possibly see to it for me?"

"Of course, sir. It's Mr Hammond isn't it?"

He acknowledged her recognition with a brief smile, brought out a pigskin wallet from the pocket of his disreputable jeans and took out a handful of notes and a business card. "Put this in with the flowers, would you?" He scribbled something on the back of the card while she counted the notes and assured him there was more than enough for a handsome arrangement.

"Don't send them up just yet," he said. "Perhaps this evening. Give her a chance to . . . well, it would be better later, I think. Oh, and nothing too formal."

"I shall see to it personally, Mr Hammond," she said, carefully putting the business card with the notes and lowering her voice confidentially. "May I say that I've always enjoyed your programmes immensely."

"Thanks," he said. "But I'm only the front man. The rest of the team is far more important."

So modest! She had always liked modesty in a man. Modesty and good manners. She cast a disdainful thought back to the uncouth, foul-mouthed rock star she'd been obliged to humour a few days since. Such a pity he couldn't take lessons from someone who wore his fame with such easy grace. Old money of course. Good family. She'd read a profile in some glossy magazine only recently.

He was already turning away. Quickly she said, "I particularly enjoyed the last series that was shown here. About the Arctic."

"Oh, yes?"

"I did so love the polar bears. They look so big and cuddly and the cubs are *so* cute, aren't they?"

"Cuddly? Cute?" He raised his eyebrows, then said dryly, "Sure, if you're not a seal about to be put on the breakfast menu." He stuffed his wallet back in his pocket. "Well, forgive me, but now I must—"

"Mother nature can be very cruel, can she not?" she put in, anxious to present herself as a sensitive, caring woman. Someone he would remember, she thought. A brief encounter. Ships that pass. He really was a most attractive man. More rugged than his television image. Taller than she'd realised. Such good bones and long, brown, sexy legs. Unlike that runt of a rock star. She hoped her lip gloss was still intact, fluttered her eyelashes and shuddered delicately. "I confess I do have to close my eyes if there is the the merest hint of blood and cruelty in these wildlife programmes."

"Do you really?" he said, sounding so interested that she could not help adding, "Of course, one knows it must go on, but I do wonder sometimes if it is necessary to show—"

"Vegetarian are you?" he asked.

"Oh, no."

He had gorgeous eyes, she thought, with the sort of long lashes wasted on a man. Well, not wasted on him. She felt her breath quicken as his gaze slid downwards to her bust, until she realised he was merely looking at her name tag.

"Well, Miss Swart – Eva," he said, raising his eyes to

17

hers again, "I do believe you've given me inspiration for a new series."

"I have?" she fluttered breathlessly.

"The private life of a rump steak, from birth to death. Including the necessary scene in the abattoir." He nodded earnestly. "How about that?"

"Well, I . . ."

"Do us all good, eh, to be reminded that steaks don't actually grow in vacuum packs on supermarket shelves, even though most of us find it convenient to believe that they do."

She realised, too late, that he was taking the mickey. A stifled sound that might have been a laugh but which changed instantly to a cough made her distressingly aware that the junior was listening. It did nothing for her composure or her temper. She strove to retrieve the situation.

"Oh, dear me, yes," she said stiffly. "We're all part of – what do you call it – the food chain?"

A slow smile curled the corners of Leon Hammond's mouth. "We surely are, Eva. It's just that we prefer all the messy business of slaughtering to be kept tidily out of sight, lest our civilised senses are offended. Think about it when you're next tucking into a delicious *filet de boeuf* eh? Thanks for seeing to the flowers for me. Nice talking to you."

A courteous nod and he was off, leaving Eva Swart feeling that somehow she had been found wanting by a man she wished to impress. She took the greatest pleasure for the rest of his shift in making the junior's life a misery by way of compensation.

When Polly returned to the suite she was sharing with her

aunt, the sitting room that linked their two bedrooms was empty. She felt a surge of relief for she knew she must look as ghastly as she felt. She'd never have got past Aunt Hes without explaining what had happened, and just now it was almost too much effort to read the note propped up against the fruit bowl on the coffee table, let alone face a battery of questions, however well meant.

> *'Gone to restore my flagging constitution in the beauty salon – facial, aromatherapy, hair-do, the works. Bliss! Should be through in time for a pre-dinner drink.'*

Polly wearily scribbled a few lines of her own, saying that she was tired after her walk and would have a long siesta before writing up some notes on the trip, and thanked heaven that Aunt Hester was such a joy to travel with. She was both independent and undemanding: perfectly content to pursue her own interests and allow Polly to follow hers within the framework of their planned schedule, and an enthusiastic and cheerful companion when they were together. When Aunt Hes returned, Polly knew she would respect her wish for privacy and she would get the few hours she needed to get her head together.

She went into her bedroom and closed the door feeling unutterably weak and weary. She dragged herself across what seemed like acres of gold carpet, dropping the camera onto a chair and kicking off her trainers as she went, and flopped down on the bed.

Blissful, blissful bed . . .

She jerked awake to the faint sound of voices and the realisation that the light was beginning to mellow to sunset. Good grief, how long had she slept? From the sound of things Aunt Hester was back on form and had, as usual, assembled a few guests for her cocktail hour.

She sat up gingerly, but despite the thick-headed feeling that sleeping in the daytime always gave her, felt much better. No faintness, no sickness. In fact for the first time since she'd fallen ill she felt properly hungry and ready for dinner.

She stood under the shower soaping her hair, then letting stinging needles of warm water cascade powerfully over her head and shoulders. Much refreshed, she was able to think more rationally about what had happened as she dried herself on fluffy yellow towels. Sure, there was still a niggle of unease about the panic attack. But she could look at it clearly, accept that it had happened and push it away to the back of her mind, as she had long since trained herself to do. As to the rest, embarrassed as she was about making such a fool of herself, she could now begin to see the funny side. That poor man! What must he have thought of her when she'd practically thrown herself into his arms.

She went to the wardrobe and pulled out the first dress that came to hand, put it on, then sat down in front of the dressing table and switched on the hairdryer. She ran the fingers of her free hand through the wet rats' tails of her hair as she swooshed the dryer about. There was no need to waste any time bothering about the impression she'd made on him. She wasn't likely to see him ever again. He'd been on his way to Durban. He'd said so. In a couple of days she'd be back in England. It was no big deal that she'd come over faint, except in her own eyes. She must look on it as a silly little incident that she would amuse Aunt Hes with later . . . Or would she? She raised her eyebrows enquiringly at her reflection in the mirror. On second thoughts, perhaps not. She still looked pale under the light tan and the rash of freckles she'd acquired in Africa. Why give Aunt Hes any cause to worry? She would if she knew. Best to be diplomatic, say nothing and avoid a lot of fuss and questions.

She put down the hairdryer, combed down her still-damp fringe and tied the rest back severely with a navy ribbon. There. Tidy enough to face whoever Aunt Hester had invited up for drinks.

She straightened her shoulders under the plain dark dress and smiled approvingly at her reflection. Good. Nobody would ever know – or need know – the upset she'd gone through. Nothing showed. All was well again.

Reassured, she slipped her feet into her comfortable black sandals and went through to meet her aunt's guests.

Half an hour later, diplomacy was not an option.

The departure of the guests – a couple of ladies Aunt Hester had met in the beauty salon, plus their husbands – had coincided with the delivery of a basket of flowers. The flowers now sat accusingly on the coffee table. Polly read the card for the second time, aware of her aunt's amused, speculative glance.

She sighed, cross that now she'd have to start explaining. "Oh, for goodness' sake don't go imagining secret assignations and phantom admirers," she said tartly. "It's just . . . well, I didn't mean to tell you because it was nothing and I didn't want you to be worried, but I had a bit of a funny turn after I'd walked along the beach . . ."

"What?" Her aunt sat bolt upright in alarm. "What kind of funny turn?"

21

"You see? I knew you'd get upset. Which is why I didn't say anything. I only went a bit faint. It was the heat and the smell of rotting shark."

"I said you were foolish to go!"

"You did. And I confess I made an error of judgement. Okay?"

"You and your photographs. This holiday was not supposed to be a marathon photographic assignment. You've enough of that in your day job."

Polly didn't rise to the bait. Aunt Hester, a self-confessed hedonist, a butterfly whose interest lay in a round of social activities, bridge parties and holidays in exotic locations claimed never to understand why Polly was so single-minded about her career. "You don't need to work yourself to a shadow, darling. All work and no play makes for a very dull person."

"And while I'm playing, someone else gets the plum assignment," Polly had said more times than she cared to remember. "You don't understand what a tough business this is, Aunt Hes. In a few years perhaps, when I've made a name for myself, I'll have time to sit around and let the commissions roll in. Not now."

"In a few years you'll have forgotten how to relax."

"If I have, I'll come to you for lessons."

"Humph. I'll believe that when it happens. I've not had much luck so far in influencing your outlook. How many years is it since I had the misfortune to find myself landed with the responsibility of such a stubborn, unruly and ungrateful niece? You were almost nine years old . . . and now you're twenty-five. Oh, God, I refuse to believe I'm that ancient."

Polly would always grin and say, "Poor old thing.

Remind me to order a walking frame for your next birthday."

In various forms the same teasing, good-natured conversation had been repeated over the years. But Polly had long come to the conclusion that behind the banter she was more like Hester Allan than her aunt would ever admit. Not in looks, that was for sure – but in a certain fundamental determination to succeed.

Each in her own way, of course.

For Hester Allan it had been anticipating – risking a very great deal in her early speculative days – the market for luxury rented accommodation for a well-heeled clientele. This insight had taken her from secretarial work in an estate agency to the ownership of several desirable properties in London and elsewhere. She had acquired, along the way, a formidable working knowledge of antiques and interior decoration and, for a brief time when she was young, a husband who not only adored her but shared her business acumen. The three-year marriage had ended abruptly with his fatal heart attack. She had never remarried, though there had been plenty of chances, and even times when she'd considered settling down. But she had grown used, she said, to independence. "Besides, what fun is there in dragging a husband along to parties or on a cruise? I hate having my style cramped. Oh, no, no, no. I have every intention of growing old singly and disgracefully." Nor did she want another husband replacing what had been the love of her life, or interfering in her business affairs, Polly surmised. For despite her smokescreen pretence of being nothing but a social butterfly, she ran her business with confidence and flair, occasionally zipping off in her current fast car to check on an agent, inspect a potential purchase, talk terms with a contractor or builder, or pleasurably search for a bargain at antique fairs.

And heaven help any human shark who saw this pretty, tiny, red-headed woman as fair game. She was perfectly capable of using her looks to her advantage, but underneath she was as tough as granite – as many an adventurer with a greedy eye on her apparent fragility and evident wealth had found to his cost.

"So how come the flowers?" her aunt said.

"A man – just a bloke who happened to be there on the beach – brought me back in his car."

"Good heavens, girl, you don't know what sort of riff-raff he could have been!"

"Look, I'm all right. Okay?"

"What was he like? Is he staying here?"

"I don't know a thing about him, except that he was on his way to Durban. I felt too grotty to ask." And too frightened.

"A responsible person, anyway, thank God," her aunt said, briskly changing tack. "In which case you should have asked him to look in for a drink. Out of courtesy."

"Come on! Courtesy was the last thing on my mind. I just wanted to crawl back here and crash out on my bed."

"Good manners, darling, are so important. People remember. One never knows when anyone, however casually met, might become important in the future." Her green eyes widened. "So, what was he like, this knight in shining armour who came to your rescue?"

Polly shrugged. "Just . . . just ordinary," she fibbed.

"Young? Old? Good looking?"

She should have made a joke of it as she usually did.

The Glass Case

Aunt Hester's interest in men was a continuous source of amusement. But today, even though the incident was settling into perspective, Polly couldn't bring herself to indulge in the ritual banter.

"I don't know. Youngish." She heard an unfamiliar note of tetchiness in her voice. "I didn't take a lot of notice."

"Really?" Surprise flickered in her aunt's green eyes. Her glance held Polly's questioningly.

"There was nothing interesting about him. Nothing at all," Polly said, quickly. Too quickly. She swallowed, looked down at the card and said with an attempt at light-heartedness that didn't quite come off, "Don't let that psychedelic imagination of yours start working overtime. Here. Read for yourself. No assignation. No promises to look me up."

Her aunt held the card at arm's length and screwed up her eyes. "'Hope you feel better soon'," her aunt read out. "How disappointing."

"You really should get your eyes tested," Polly said sternly, seizing an opportunity to change the subject. "You definitely need reading glasses."

"Me? Nothing wrong with my eyes!"

"Oh, yeah? Just that you need longer arms, is it? One of these days, Aunt Hes, you'll have to stop pretending that you're still thirty-nine and own up to being over fifty."

"Wash your mouth out, girl!"

"Fifty-three's not old these days, for heaven's sake," Polly said, relaxing, beginning to smile now that she'd diverted attention away from herself. But her aunt wasn't listening. She'd turned the card over and was staring at it open-mouthed.

"Polly! Is this right? Or can there be two of them?"

"What do you mean?"

"Was it really *the* Leon Hammond who rescued you and sent you flowers?"

"Who?"

"Give me strength! You know, does those wildlife programmes."

"I hardly watch television . . ." she began. Then stopped. The name clicked into her mind. Her mind spun it round. Fixed the name to the face of the man on the beach. "Oh," she said.

"Penny dropped has it?"

Polly chewed her lip, thinking. Had her subconscious sensed something vaguely familiar about those hawkish features? Had that sense of familiarity set off a reaction in her weak and barely functioning state, which had sent her senses off on a wild canter in an entirely wrong direction?

"He . . . he was different," she protested. "Looked like . . . like, I don't know," she floundered. "Rough looking . . . I'd never have guessed."

"Obviously," her aunt said, heaving a dramatic sigh. "But what a missed opportunity. Mind, you could ring up and thank him for the flowers when you get back." She brightened. "There's no address, unfortunately, but there's a London number. Charles wouldn't object, would he? He's far too cold a fish. Has he worked up to kissing you goodnight yet?"

"Aunt Hes!" Polly growled. "That's enough. Forget it. I won't have you teasing me about Charles. I know you don't mean it but I'm not in the mood."

"Who says I don't mean it? But okay, okay." Hester put her empty glass and the card on the table. "Subject closed. For now." She eyed the arrangement of purple and orange strelitzias standing to attention amid bayonet

26

spikes of foliage of a particularly virulent shade of green and clicked her tongue disapprovingly. "I will, though, say one last word on the subject of Leon Hammond. He may be big in the wildlife conservation movement and I am very grateful for his rescue of you, but his choice of flowers for a poorly person is most peculiar. Enough to give anyone a setback."

"It's the thought that counts," Polly said firmly, but was promptly overcome with giggles. "It does all look a bit, well, aggressive, doesn't it?"

"Very predatory. Mind you don't get too close, or it might bite. Now come on, let's go in search of dinner. I'm ravenous."

She was ready for home, Polly realised, as she lay in bed that night, listening to the rhythmic boom and rush of the surf in the darkness beyond the open window. It had been a wonderful three weeks, but now she felt a sudden, sharp nostalgia for the misty, gentle colours of an English November day after the heat and brilliance of southern Africa. She was itching to see how all the films she'd taken would turn out. And there was Charles. She was so looking forward to seeing him again. Of course she was. She yawned, tugging the sheet over her shoulders. He'd be there waiting at Heathrow. Dear Charles . . .

The dream – the nightmare – took her by surprise. It was so long since it had happened that she was overwhelmed before she was able to gather her wits and force herself to wake up before it took hold. She slid down, down into the place of shadows. Monstrous, threatening shadows that coiled about her, sinuous as snakes. She was trapped. She was always trapped and alone. She knew she must force herself to go from the writhing darkness to where the glimmer of light promised safety. But *they* were behind her, reaching out with clawing fingers and her feet seemed to be mired in mud, so that each step was a slow-motion travesty of movement. Then the voices began, shouting, screaming, seeming to split her skull. She wanted them to stop, wanted to end this violation by sound, but the noise went on and on. And when she crawled into the light, she knew that safety was an illusion. They were still there, behind her, in the scarlet-tinged darkness, wanting her, reaching for her, pulling her down . . . down into the mire.

She surfaced, sobbing and struggling, the sheet coiled tightly round her waist, her nightdress soaked with sweat.

The sense of menace was so vivid that she cowered back against the pillows until she was properly awake, until sanity returned, until her heartbeat calmed and was lost in the sound of the surf.

She wanted Charles.

She fought her way out of the bedclothes, switched on the light and scrabbled for her diary. The phone was slippy with the sweat from her hand. Somehow she jabbed out the long string of numbers and half a world away the phone purred. Only then did she think about the time. Was it the middle of the night? No, no. Twelve twenty-seven here. Knock off what? Two hours? Three? The phone rang on. Where was he? She just wanted to hear his voice. Calm, sane, kind Charles, who loved her. Who would free her from the lingering clutch of the nightmare.

He wasn't there. He'd not even switched on his answerphone. Even the sound of his recorded voice would have given her the illusion of comfort, of reassurance. After a couple of minutes she put down the receiver.

The Glass Case

She needed a drink.

She crept into the sitting room. The light from the open bedroom door was enough for her to negotiate the dark shapes of furniture. She took a miniature of brandy from the bar fridge, unscrewed the cap and managed to stop herself choking as she drank a mouthful neat. She took another swig.

The bloody man! Leon Hammond. It was his fault. He'd set off all this . . . this stuff. Him and his piratical looks. She wished she'd never clapped eyes on him. She wished she'd collapsed in the bushes and got over her faint by herself, and he'd driven off and never known she was there!

In the fan of yellow light from the bedroom door the clump of flowers stuck rigidly in the florist's basket looked even more venomously predatory than they had before. Bird of paradise flowers. Pterodactyls more like. Orange beaks wide, ready to peck and rip and destroy.

She shuddered, tipped back the last of the brandy and crossed soft-footed to the coffee table.

She picked up the basket and carried it across to the glass double door. She drew back the long silky curtain far enough for her to unlock the door and slide it open. Then she stepped outside on to the balcony, dropped the basket to the floor and kicked it roughly with her bare foot into the furthest corner.

Somehow that one small act of vandalism against the innocent flowers seemed to revive her. That or the brandy hitting the right spot. She leant against the balcony railing for a moment, breathing in the mingled aromas of salt and seaweed, and the waft of some perfumed bush in the garden below. The sky was black silk crusted with a diamante extravagance of stars. If only Charles were here. But he wasn't.

With a sigh she went back inside. She drew the curtains back with a defiant swish, then went back to bed and slept without dreaming.

Two

D urban airport was busy. Polly and her aunt were engulfed in a mass of passengers and luggage trolleys before Polly spied a gap and zoomed past a group of Indian women – all fluttering saris and clashing bangles as they tearfully embraced each other – towards the luggage check-in, her aunt close behind.

Hester Allan was a hopeless travel junkie. "I love it all, darling. Even being stranded with four hundred others in the remotest airport with wooden benches and one working loo. I see a plane, a train, a boat and I want to be on it."

Apart from a couple of trips with Aunt Hes to a cottage she rented in the south of France – and that had been years ago while Polly was in her teens – she hadn't been abroad since that last fateful trip to the Middle East when she was nine. It was her parents' work – they were archaeologists – that had taken them abroad, and she had joined them in the school holidays when any travel delays had seemed achingly dull.

But there were no delays this evening. Polly smiled to herself as they boarded the plane to be greeted by the steward and shown to their comfortable seats in Business Class. Despite her claim to enjoy any aspect of travel, Aunt Hester invariably avoided the cramped conditions

31

in Economy, quite often travelling First and taking all the extra attention as her due. Polly would have been quite content to fly squashed up in the cheapest seats but Aunt Hester had insisted.

"Darling, I can afford it, so why not? I want to spoil you for once. This holiday is my treat, a long overdue treat. I've never forgiven you for refusing any sort of a party when you were eighteen and again when you were twenty-one. Never mind informing me that you didn't need or want fripperies, only a contribution, a *small* contribution – if I felt it necessary – towards buying an enlarger or some smelly chemicals or something equally obnoxious. Impudent little madam! Well, you've had your way long enough. Now it's my turn to lay down the law. You need a holiday. It's years since you had a decent break, and I'd like a companion on this particular trip. If I'm to meet hungry lions or charging elephants, I'd prefer to do so in the company of my nearest and dearest."

"Get away," Polly had said, laughing. "No lion would dare to charge you for fear you'd thump him on the nose with those knuckleduster rings of yours. But since you ask me so prettily, I've a mind to be persuaded."

As the lights of Durban wheeled away beneath them and the plane set its course across Africa, Polly remembered the last three weeks with pleasure. Aunt Hes had given her a wonderfully generous present. A kaleidoscope of images flickered in her mind: the sweep of thunderheads billowing up into the intense blue sky, small children herding goats under flame trees, dusty villages amid plantations of maize and banana where the wilderness had been tamed.

And the untamable: a pride of bloodied lions snarling over the entrails of a zebra, a herd of elephant threading its majestic way amid a skitter of warthogs, grazing impala with their glossy honey and brown pelts, ambling giraffes. The game parks had been a revelation and a joy. If she had managed to capture something of the magic of these beasts in their natural surroundings it would be a bonus. But wildlife photography was something new to her. She was used to studio work or buildings, inanimate objects that could be assessed carefully from all angles and photographed at a precisely measured moment when the conditions and the light showed up proportions, character and interesting features to the best advantage.

Wildlife photography was very different. In one way it was not unlike portrait photography which she had abandoned early in her career, feeling inhibited by the expectations of those who demanded that they be portrayed as dashing or winsome or elegant or whatever flattering image they had of themselves. She had always wanted to delve deeper than the superficial image – to reveal, through the lens, the true spirit of the inner person, flattering or not. It was almost the same problem with animals. It would have been easy to make them into cliché calender shots entitled Regal Lion or Mischievous Baboon. To capture the essence of a particular beast was something else. She had known what she'd wanted to achieve, but there were so many variables – the quality of light, the constant movement of the animals, the sheer lottery of being at a particular place at the right moment – that it was impossible to say whether she'd managed to catch those elusive, magical seconds when everything came together to make the perfect shot.

If she had, just once, it would be the finishing touch to a wonderful trip.

*   *   *

From his seat at the rear of the compartment Leon Hammond eyed the pair of seats ahead and to the right of him. Unless she leaned forward, all he could see of the Burton woman from here was her elbow on the armrest. Common sense told him that was enough. There was no need to take their acquaintance any further. He was too tired, anyway. It had been a heavy couple of days with lectures, meetings, the inevitable and necessary socialising. Then a mad dash to get to the airport and the traffic hold-up that had meant he'd been practically the last person to board.

He'd seen her straight away. She'd been standing up to take off her black jacket as he was being shown to his seat. She hadn't looked round. She'd been talking to the person next to her. The aunt she'd travelled with, he supposed. She was still talking as she sat down again, her face, in profile, animated and smiling as he'd not seen it before.

"More coffee, Mr Hammond?"

"Thanks." The steward refilled his cup and moved on.

She'd recovered. That was all he needed – or wished – to know. He'd finish his coffee, get out his laptop and write up his notes before he got his head down. Forget about her.

He watched the steward approach her seat. No more coffee for her. Sensible girl. No overload of caffeine to keep her awake. Sensibly dressed for travel in black trousers and T-shirt.

Sensible, now. Not then, though. Not in that astonishing moment when she'd looked at him with sheer bloody terror in her eyes. As though he'd metamorphosed into the devil himself. For a minute he'd thought she was going to fling herself out of the car. He'd even eased up on the accelerator as he'd seen her hand go for the door handle, convinced she was about to hurl herself away from him and on to the concrete drive. He'd been ready to grab her if she'd tried.

Then, somehow, she'd taken control of herself. She was shaking so hard, poor girl, he could almost feel it through the car's suspension. When he took her elbow to help her into the hotel he could feel the effort it took her not to pull away, as though his touch brought back echoes of that same terror and revulsion.

It was nothing personal. How could it be? They'd never met before. It was, he thought wryly, certainly a novelty for a woman to react to him in that particular way: light years from the skin-shrivelling sycophancy – the downside of having a public persona – that he sometimes had to put up with. Perhaps that was why he was intrigued, wanting to know why.

Intrigued enough to follow it up? He thoughtfully took a mouthful of coffee. Sooner or later she'd probably spot him anyway. Then what? Another fit of the shakes? A bit tough on her in such a public place. Perhaps it was better not risk any sort of scene. If she was prone to collapsing in a faint he ought to make his presence known while she was sitting down. And with an eye to the whereabouts of the steward in case ice cubes were needed.

He'd give her chance to digest her dinner then make a move.

Decision taken, he sat back to finish his coffee and to wait for an appropriate moment.

"Miss Burton? I thought it was you. How are you?"

Polly looked up and froze. She'd been idly glancing at the list of films available on video and wondering whether to view something or finish her paperback. Aunt Hester already had her video switched on and, headset clamped round her ears, was lost in some action-packed drama.

"You certainly look better," he said. "I take it that you've made a full recovery."

She managed a stiff little nod. A hesitation, then, "Thank you, yes."

He smiled down at her. "Quite a coincidence meeting up again like this," he said easily, as though he was completely unaware that she was sitting like a frozen lump, trying to control her breathing. "I only caught the flight by the skin of my teeth otherwise we might have bumped into each other in the departure lounge. I'm sitting at the back there."

"Oh," she said faintly. "Yes. Quite a coincidence."

"And this will be your aunt," he said. "You mentioned you were travelling with her."

"Did I?" She dragged her thoughts into some kind of order. She was being ridiculous. She wasn't ill now and there was nothing about his appearance this evening to cause panic. The stubble had gone, he'd had a haircut and his blue eyes held nothing but warmth. Though he was jacketless and had pulled his tie loose for comfort, the expensive-looking cream silk shirt and brown slacks made him look nothing like the T-shirted brigand of the beach.

Except for those hard-boned features, the hawkish nose . . . No, no, don't think like that . . .

"I daresay our previous conversation is all a bit of a blur," he said. "You were hardly with it most of the time."

"I guess so. I'm sorry."

"No problem."

"The flowers," Polly said, remembering her manners. "Thank you. It was a very kind thought."

He made a small disparaging gesture with one large tanned hand. "My pleasure." He seemed about to say something more, but hesitated and then said, briskly, "Well, I won't keep you. I just wanted to say hello."

He was going. Thank goodness. She'd be able to breathe properly again.

But, to her dismay, at that moment Aunt Hester realised that it wasn't the steward engaging her niece in conversation, but a very different order of person. Her eyes widened in surprise and pleasure. The headset was removed in an instant.

"It's Mr Hammond, isn't it?" She held out her hand. "Hester Allan, Polly's aunt. I'm so pleased that I'm able to thank you personally for rescuing my niece the other day."

"Glad I was able to help," he said.

"One hears such tales . . . Well, all I can say is, thank heaven she met a responsible person."

The conversational pleasantries passed back and forth over Polly's head. She noted, with a sigh, that Aunt Hester had assumed her man-eating mode. For heaven's sake, there must be twenty years difference in their ages! She was laying on the full charm: green eyes wide and sparkling, small be-ringed hand clinging just a fraction too long to his. No man was safe when she set her mind to it. Polly had chuckled many times over similar performances. She didn't feel like laughing now.

"I have to say, Mr Hammond," Hester was saying conspiratorially, "that one is often disappointed when one sees celebrities in the flesh, but you're much better looking than on television."

Heaven forfend! Blatant flattery! Why didn't he just clear off instead of standing there like a grinning booby?

Aunt Hester was flirting with him. Outrageously. Couldn't he see that? Yes he could, she thought irritably. He was responding with all the expertise of a man accustomed to it. Well, she wasn't prepared to sit here and watch them charm each other's socks off. Artificial claptrap.

"Excuse me," she said, reaching for her toilet bag and getting to her feet, "If I might pass . . ."

He hastily stepped aside. Aunt Hester patted the armrest. "Do sit down if you can spare a minute, Mr Hammond."

Polly turned her back on them and strode to the toilet compartment where she spent ages cleaning her teeth and washing her face, hoping that by the time she was through Leon Hammond would be back in his own seat. She dragged the tight ribbon from her hair and tugged the comb through it. It had grown while she'd been away. She'd trim the ends herself, as she usually did, when she got home. Never mind Aunt Hester's nagging, which she'd had plenty of this holiday, that she should have a decent cut.

"What ever for?" Polly always said. "I'm comfortable with my hair as it is. It's easy to manage and that's what matters."

"But you could make so much more of yourself."

Only yesterday Aunt Hes had had a go at her over the dress she'd been wearing for dinner each evening. "Not that dull old thing again," she'd groaned. "Honestly, darling, you've no dress sense at all. It's the wrong length, the wrong cut and completely out of date."

"I don't like frills and fuss."

"There is a happy medium between dressing like a Christmas tree and never venturing beyond the dreary and dismal."

"You've got the looks in the family, Aunt Hes," she'd protested. "I know my limits. I'd look ridiculous swanning around in fancy gear."

"Rubbish. A change of hairstyle, a make-over . . ."

She'd laughed. "All the make-up and swanky haircuts in the world would never make me pretty."

"Pretty? Not in the conventional sense . . ."

"Well then."

"Stop interrupting and listen to someone who knows what she's talking about," Hester said severely. "If you'd get rid of that ghastly sheepdog fringe, the world would be able to see what beautiful eyes you've got. Not bad bone structure, either. *And* you've the height and figure many would die for. You could look supremely elegant and classy if you put your mind to it, and I find it so frustrating that you won't even try! I'm sure if your mother were alive she'd have brought you up to make the best of yourself."

"I don't want to hear," Polly said, suddenly tense. "I'm nothing like my mother. I'm not beautiful. I know that. And I've no interest in dolling myself up. Now can we change the subject, please?"

She stared at her reflection now. Elegant? Classy? She couldn't honestly understand what Aunt Hes was on about. There was certainly nothing remarkable about the face that stared back at her from the mirror. A frown drew down her eyebrows, her mouth was tight and set, the rusty hair – a dull colour, far from the flamboyant auburn of Hester's – newly released from its ribbon sprang out boisterously round her face and neck. Eyes not too bad, she admitted reluctantly, after a moment's consideration. The colour was nice. A sort of greeny-brown flecked with gold. But they weren't wide and dramatic enough, in her opinion, to lend any sort of distinction to her face.

Nothing to attract Leon Hammond's attention, she thought. Then pulled herself up short. Good grief, she was getting paranoid. He wasn't following her, for heaven's sake. It was pure chance that they were on the same flight.

She straightened her shoulders under the comfortably baggy T-shirt. She nodded, cheerfully enough, at her reflection. Panic over. She was okay. Tomorrow everything would be back to normal. She'd be home. Far away from the technicolour holiday world of Africa. Sane and safe, back to real life.

And now she'd better get out of here before someone started hammering on the door.

She was pleased to see that Leon Hammond had vacated her seat. Unfortunately, he hovered in the aisle when he saw her coming. She pinned a bright social smile on her face.

"Time to get my head down," she said lightly.

He was holding a book in his hand. He held it up.

"I mentioned to your aunt that, interesting as my trip's been, I now have the tedious business of writing up my notes," he said. "So she insisted I take this to read instead."

"There's absolutely no obligation," Polly said, feeling embarrassed and glaring at her aunt, who smiled back blithely.

"'*A Heritage of British Follies*,'" he read from the jacket. "'Text by Charles R. Gregson. Photographs by Polly Burton.' Mm. Interesting."

"No need to be polite, either. My aunt's a bit over-enthusiastic, sometimes."

"I'm not being polite," he said, flicking through the pages. "Some superb photographs in here." He looked at her. "Must have taken some time to get all this together."

"Over two years, on and off. Fitting in trips around other work."

"Your idea? Or Gregson's."

"It's Charles's hobby. He's an architect. He's seen too many of these old follies fallen into ruin or knocked down for housing estates or road schemes. Over the years he's kept a private record. I thought it was something that might appeal to a wider audience."

"So it was your idea," he said.

"Charles is the expert," she said. "I just thought a collection like this might contribute something towards preserving what's left." She shrugged. "Whether it will have any effect is another matter. People need houses, factories. Why preserve a heap of crumbling Victorian stonework in the middle of a field that's wanted for a new estate, or a useless tower that's blocking a town bypass?"

He smiled. "It's the same problem that the environmental lobby and wildlife conservationists face. The price of a piece of woodland with its diverse flora and fauna, set against the power of the developers."

She shied away from the inference that they might have something in common and said firmly, "Well, I am really rather tired. If you will excuse me . . ."

"Of course. Sleep well."

He moved away and Polly settled thankfully back into her seat.

It was a long night. Polly dozed fitfully, disturbing little dreams jerking her awake from time to time. She was glad when the lights went up and she could go and wash the sleep from her gritty eyes. She wished, for once, that she had Aunt Hester's knack of managing to look fresh and well groomed at all times, even after a night of travel.

Leon Hammond was at her elbow, book in hand, as breakfast was cleared. Aunt Hester had disappeared to the loo. For some reason she felt pleased to see that he looked somewhat tired and dishevelled himself, the silk shirt crumpled and dark shadows under his eyes.

"I never sleep much on night flights," he said, as though he guessed her thoughts. He smiled. "You seemed well away, though, when I passed in the small hours."

"Did I really?" she said coldly, not liking the idea at all that he'd been spying on her.

"You were snoring, actually," he said, his blue eyes alive with amusement. "But very gently and in a most ladylike manner. As for me, the book should have helped me to nod off, but no such luck. It was boring enough."

"Oh?"

"Don't look so affronted. The photographs were excellent. It was the text that left a lot to be desired. Can't say I go a bomb on Charles Gregson's style. Amateurish and long-winded in the extreme."

"That's just your opinion, Mr Hammond."

"You've had good reviews, then?"

"That's my advance copy. The book came out while I've been away."

He shook his head. "Don't expect to make a million."

"I don't," she said, bristling with indignation. "That wasn't the reason Charles and I did the book. I told you, Charles is an authority on his subject."

"Pity he couldn't put it across, then. If I may, I'd like to offer you some advice. The next time you collaborate

42

with someone, make sure his or her standards are up to yours."

"Thank you for your opinion, but—"

"Look at this photograph. And this." He was riffling enthusiastically through the book, ignoring her, stopping here and there to jab a finger at the pages. "These are terrific. I especially like this one." He held the book open. "It almost knocks you out with the sense of desolation. The sweep of the empty moor and this ruin, stark against the bank of storm clouds. All in moody black and white. Perfect medium."

She was taken aback. Of all the photographs in the book this was her favourite. It had taken her two days to get the effect she'd wanted. Two days of getting soaked hanging about the Yorkshire moors, waiting for the rain to stop. And it nearly hadn't made it into the book. Both Charles and their editor at the publishing house had preferred a colour shot she'd taken before the rain set in. She'd had quite a struggle to persuade them. But she'd dug her heels in, knowing in her bones that this was the one photograph that, to her, made the whole exercise worthwhile.

"If the book does well," Leon Hammond said, "it'll be your photographs that sell it. I'd bet a pound to a penny." He looked into her eyes. His were clear and honest. "I'm sorry to be so blunt. I'm sure this Charles Gregson is a great guy, but as a writer he's no asset to you. Think about it if there's talk of another book. Do you have a contract with the publisher?"

"An option on the next book if we come up with another suitable idea. That's all."

"Well, don't rush into another collaboration. That's my advice."

She didn't know what to say. She couldn't help feeling

pleased that he'd been so complimentary about the pictures but knew she should have retained some indignation on Charles' behalf. But somehow it had gone away. Perhaps, at the back of her mind, she'd always known the truth of it. When she'd first read the manuscript, although she'd been respectful of the work Charles had put in and of his wide knowledge of the subject, it had been an effort to wade through. She'd put her indifferent feelings down to her own feeble taste in literature, which mostly ran to fat novels with lots of pace that carried her briefly into the colourful life of characters remote from her everyday existence. She'd told herself that she had no discrimination. But now, it seemed, neither did Leon Hammond. Or rather, he confirmed what she had sensed about Charles's writing from the first. Not that she had any intention of admitting it. She couldn't be that disloyal.

He closed the book, smoothed his hand over the dust jacket.

"Excellent cover shot, too," he said. "This one had to be in colour, didn't it? Just look at that wonderfully ornate shell grotto and that mad riot of purple wisteria scrambling all over it." He smiled at her. "I think I could have forgiven Charles Gregson if he'd launched into equally purple prose to describe it. At least it might have conveyed his enthusiasm to the reader. Instead of which—"

"Mr Hammond," she began.

"Leon, please."

"Mr Hammond," she repeated, "I do appreciate your comments on my photographs, but I think you're quite wrong about the text. The publisher was most enthusiastic."

"An old school chum of Gregson's, was he?"

"No he wasn't," she said tartly, suppressing the thought that the commissioning editor was one of Charles's regular golfing partners. "And in any case, I think publishing's too tough a business these days to survive by the old boy network."

"True. Then I'd hazard a guess that the editor was shrewd enough, even if he didn't say as much, to see that your photographs and the snappy captions – yours? I thought so – were strong enough to carry the book to a wide audience. Charles Gregson's name may be in large letters on the title page, but for my money you'll be the one who deserves the credit if you get into the best-seller lists."

The plane had been losing height. Now the seat belt sign pinged on. They were on the final approach and the plane dipped suddenly from the brilliant blue and gold of early morning into thick grey cloud, lurching a little so that as Leon Hammond handed Polly the book, he had to clutch the back of her seat to keep his balance. The book slipped and they both made a grab for it. His hand came down firmly on hers, holding both it and the book for a second.

"I'd better get back to my seat and get my stuff together," he said quietly. "But do think about what I've said, won't you? About future collaboration?"

She nodded because there was nothing else she could do. She wanted to tell him to get lost, him and his opinions, but that foolish breathlessness had caught her again. She could think of nothing, for a panicky moment, but the pressure of his hand, the way he stood so threateningly close . . .

He released her hand, moved back slightly, not taking his eyes off her face.

"Okay?" he said gently.

She swallowed and managed to say in a voice devoid of expression, "I can't say that I'm particularly concerned with your opinion, Mr Hammond. But thank you for your interest."

Oh, God, why didn't he go?

After a moment, without another word, he did.

Curiouser and curiouser.

Leon Hammond buckled his seat belt and stared out at the thick, enveloping cloud. The plane bumped and shuddered on its descent. A few minutes more and they'd be landing at Heathrow. He glanced at his watch – spot on time – then found his gaze drawn inexorably to where she sat. Nothing of her visible now, as though she'd tucked herself tightly down into her seat to prevent his glimpsing even an inch of elbow.

Or maybe she was phobic about air travel. Plenty of people were.

He pondered this, rejected it.

It wasn't fear of a crash landing that bothered Polly Burton. Her reaction had only been a shadow of that first time, and she'd recovered quickly now that she wasn't weakened and made vulnerable by illness. But reaction there had been. To him.

He wasn't sure whether to be glad or sorry that he'd got involved with her.

Involved? Was he?

Only temporarily. Once he was off the plane that would be it. He didn't need to know any more than he did already. That she was prickly and defensive and difficult. But underneath? Very different. Certainly clever and talented. For the rest . . . ? Grudgingly he admitted

46

that he was still curious about whatever trauma lay at the root of her reaction. And he was a man who seriously disliked loose ends and enigmas.

He forced himself to think of her objectively. Too tall, too thin, too ordinary. Tried to tell himself that he'd no time or inclination to bother about her.

But he did have the inclination and he could make the time.

He swore under his breath. What was it about her that had got under his skin in such an irritating fashion?

But he didn't really need to ask.

She had the most beautiful eyes. He'd looked into their slanting, browny-green, gold-specked depths and was captivated by the thought of how they regarded the world. Those beautiful eyes transformed her undistinguished features. And they looked out with a vision that was lucid and imaginative and which marked her work as a photographer as very special indeed.

A yawn overtook him. He'd play it by ear. Try and find some opportunity to draw her out before they parted. Some point of contact. Play it light and easy. And if she wouldn't – couldn't – respond? He'd have to think again.

The plane broke free of the cloud. It emerged into the gloomy damp London morning, lined up for the runway and landed with the gentlest of bumps. Polly listened to Aunt Hester outlining her plans for the coming weeks.

"I shall go to the Torquay flat today, of course, but I shall be back in London to do my Christmas shopping before crowds get too hectic. We'll get together for dinner and a show then, shall we?"

"Great," she said absently.

The compartment was full, yet every nerve in her body seemed aware of only one person. What was he doing? Was he staring out at the cloud whisking in dense tendrils past the window? Or was he looking down the aisle, spying on her?

"Such a charming man," Aunt Hester said, reverting to the topic Polly hoped she'd already worried into oblivion. "I can't get over how pleasant and unassuming he was. Not a bit like some well-known people I've met – full of their own importance and with super-inflated egos to match."

"I don't know how you can possibly tell from a few minutes conversation," Polly said irritably. "He's probably a complete bore when you get to know him."

"Oh, it's not only me, darling. That article I read . . ."

"Not again," Polly groaned.

"He's very well liked," Hester said unabashed. "And his views on conservation are well respected, too."

"Saint Leon," Polly muttered.

"You're being unfair, darling."

"You told me yourself he'd been a brat when he was young. What elevated him to sainthood? A bolt of lightning? Conversion on the road to Damascus?"

"He mixed with a wild crowd. He admitted it in the article. He had too much money at his disposal. Then he grew up. I suspect his divorce had a lot to do with it. Once his jet-setting wife was out of the picture he came to his senses pretty rapidly. Reading between the lines I'd say his wife was a bitchy beauty with very little between the ears." Her rings glittered as she waved her hand. "Teenage marriages are risky ventures. Oh, I know there are exceptions, like your own parents. They never had eyes for anyone else from the time they were sixteen.

48

They made a go of it despite all the doom-mongers. The odds were certainly stacked against them, what with marriage when they were up at Oxford and a baby at twenty. But they were very determined people and very much in love. I dare say the young Hammonds didn't have so much going for them, despite having plenty of money. Ah, here we are."

"Thank goodness," Polly said, taking her time about unclipping her seat belt and getting into her jacket. A stewardess brought their coats and hand luggage and she slowly and carefully checked that she had everything. She wasn't going to hurry. Let him get swept away with the first rush of people out of the plane, never to be seen again.

Her luck was out. He was waiting for them by the door. Her heart sank. He included both of them in his warm smile, volunteering to carry Aunt Hester's bag, an offer she promptly accepted. Then, keeping up a cheerful flow of conversation, he accompanied them through immigration and to the luggage bay where he fetched trolleys and was exceedingly and nerve-rackingly helpful.

Polly gritted her teeth and kept aloof, grateful that at least the other two seemed more than ready to chat to each other and ignore her. It wouldn't be long now. The carousel would soon fill with baggage. Maybe theirs would be first and they could rush away and lose him. But it took an age and, of course, his case arrived promptly and he insisted on waiting until he'd hauled theirs off the carousel, stacked their trolley and strolled with them through the green *'Nothing to Declare'* channel.

"I always feel guilty, don't you?" he remarked as they walked past the watchful customs officials. "As though I've a fortune in contraband hidden in my left sock."

Aunt Hester laughed. "I always say the same, don't I, Polly"

"Yes," she said shortly, keeping her gaze fixed on the barriers ahead, searching for the one blessedly familiar face she most wanted to see.

"We must have built-in guilt complexes," Leon said. "How about you?" He turned towards Polly as he spoke. She wished he wouldn't look at her in that considering kind of way. Watchful.

"Can't say I've given it much thought."

"No?"

"No."

"Ah, you're far too sensible to make imaginative mistakes like that." Aunt Hester had moved ahead of them now. People pushed past, the crowds at the barrier waved and called out. In the bustle, quite suddenly, she seemed to be marooned on an island of silence into which he said, softly, "And yet you look at me as though I were a spider you'd found in your bath. What's that about Polly?"

"I like spiders."

"But you don't like me."

She swallowed. Her hands had broken into a cold sweat on the handle of the trolley. "This is a ridiculous conversation."

"Ridiculous? Don't you mean upsetting?"

"What on earth have I got to be upset about?"

"You tell me."

"There is absolutely nothing to tell." She spoke slowly and clearly, as though to a inquisitive, irritating child. "And you, Mr Hammond, are . . . are . . ."

"Yes?"

". . . becoming a nuisance. I was grateful for your help when I was ill, but there's a word for someone who . . . who harasses people. I'd prefer not to have to apply it to you, so please go away. Now. This minute."

"Suppose I don't?"

"Look. I refuse to stay here bandying words. We met. You were kind. That's it. Goodbye."

"But not forever."

"What do you mean?"

"I think we ought to meet up again."

"I don't think so."

He smiled. "When I make up my mind to do something, I'm not easily put off." His tone was light, conversational.

Indignation and alarm churned in her mind. What had Aunt Hes said about inflated egos? She'd been way out over this one. Arrogant sod.

"Tough," she said, and made to thrust the trolley past him. His hand came down over hers.

"My car's outside. Can I at least offer you a lift?"

"We're being met."

"Pity. I'm sure your aunt would approve." His eyes glinted wickedly, inviting her to share his amusement at his accurate assessment of Aunt Hes. "It's a Jag. New model, very comfortable."

"Please remove your hand from my trolley." She tried to wriggle her fingers away but he didn't budge.

"So who's meeting you?"

"It's none of your business."

He looked past her to where Hester, already at the end of the barrier, was greeting a distinguished-looking, grey-haired man.

"Ah, I see. Looks a sober and responsible citizen." He

51

smiled down at her. "Forgive me, but I didn't quite believe you. I thought you were making excuses."

"Why on earth should I?"

"Because your irrational feelings about me seem to be colouring your judgement." He loosened his grip slightly but didn't release her hand. It seemed, for a moment, that he might try to prise her fingers from the trolley handle, enfold it in his own. But he didn't. He just said quietly, "My apologies," and gave her hand a little, encouraging pat. Almost, she thought indignantly, as though she were a pet dog or cat he was aiming to soothe.

Well, she wasn't soothed. Far from it. She snatched her hand away

"Goodbye, Mr Hammond," she said.

"Au revoir, perhaps?"

"Definitely goodbye," she said, stepping briskly forward.

He matched her steps with his long, loping stride. They both looked towards the grey-haired man who lifted his hand in a discreet wave at Polly's approach, a welcoming smile etched on his finely drawn features.

"Your father?" Leon enquired.

She looked up at him. For the first time she realised that she had just the weapon to wipe that smug smile off his face, to free herself from this overbearing, dangerous man whom she wished never, ever to clap eyes on again. Her escape route was clear and she felt a surge of relief.

"Not my father, no," she said, clearly and politely. She didn't flinch now from the too-perceptive blue glance, knowing her defences to be secure and impregnable. "Do let me introduce you to the man I shall soon be marrying. I'm sure he'd like to thank you personally for your concern and kindness."

The Glass Case

She held up her left hand so that the diamond on her third finger glittered in the light. "I should very much like you to meet the man who bought me this ring. My fiancé, Charles Gregson."

Three

"Welcome home, Polly." Charles smiled warmly and kissed her cheek.

She was so glad to see his dear and familiar face that her answering smile and hug were extra enthusiastic.

Charles looked pleased but faintly embarrassed. Polly's spirits soared happily. If anything was guaranteed to restore her sense of normality, so recently disturbed by Leon Hammond's unwanted attentions, it was seeing Charles again.

Merely by being his reserved and gentlemanly self he brought order to her chaotic emotions. She was home. Her feet were back on the ground. She could forget all about the unfortunate episode with Leon Hammond. She could even – with her hand tucked securely into the crook of Charles's elbow – watch with complete equanimity as Aunt Hester made the introductions and explanations and Charles murmured courteous thanks to Leon for looking after them both.

She was delighted to see that the buccaneer was momentarily discomfited. He had looked from her to Charles with disbelief written all over his face. Perhaps, she thought gleefully, he was remembering how harsh he'd been in his criticism of Charles's writing. Good. Served him right for being so presumptuous. Unfortunately, he quickly recovered and, after a few polite words with Charles, set himself to a prolonged farewell with Aunt Hes. She, of course, played up shamefully as telephone numbers were exchanged.

"You must promise to look me up if you're ever in south Devon," she said, gazing up at him, her green eyes twinkling mischievously. "I mix a mean Tequila Sunrise. Be warned – it's been known to make strong men quail. But if you think you can take. it—"

"Nothing I like better than a challenge," he said, grinning.

"And nothing I like better than a man with a reckless streak."

"Then here's to an assignation in Torquay."

Polly could stand no more of it. She was also uncomfortably aware that Charles was beginning to assume the pained expression that he so often wore when in Aunt Hester's company.

She tugged his arm and he took a firm grip on the trolley. They both threw 'time we were going' looks at Aunt Hester. And, at last, Leon Hammond seemed to take the hint.

He moved off briskly, turned one last time to give a cheerful wave that Polly decided to ignore, and disappeared into the milling crowd. Never to be seen again, she fervently hoped.

Now she was free to turn all her attention to Charles.

Charles drove carefully and precisely through the frantic traffic. Polly relaxed beside him, welcoming each glimpse of the London landmarks she knew so well. Home. Even on such a drizzly, grey morning there was enormous pleasure in being back where she belonged, with people she loved.

They threaded through the back roads towards Hampstead and turned into the square of houses set around a tiny, railed park. Charles lived at the far end, a tall, plain-fronted house in a late-Georgian terrace, the interior of which precisely reflected Charles's architectural style: minimalist and functional, with the emphasis on quality materials and clean, stark lines. The distinctive stamp Polly had seen in all the buildings he'd designed was impressed on his personal surroundings: smooth unclut-tered surfaces, a feeling of space and airiness, understated colours.

"Like living in an upmarket public convenience," Aunt Hester had once muttered, her own taste running to haphazard and expensive clutter that conveyed an overall impression of opulence. The antithesis of everything Charles admired.

They sat in the oyster-grey dining room to eat the cold lunch prepared by Mrs Sheppard, Charles's housekeeper. Stiffly starched white linen, immaculately plain silver cut-lery and white china were set on the polished black surface of the dining table. The only concession to ornament was one perfectly placed and spotlit Chinese painting on silk of white egrets in a grey landscape on the wall opposite the window.

The decor cut no ice with Aunt Hester.

"What you need in here, Charles," she said, nibbling a sliver of smoked salmon, "are some of those brilliantly coloured handmade wool rugs we saw – where was it Polly? Oh, some arty-crafty place in Nairobi."

"Very ethnic," he said dryly.

"Plain fitted carpet in a room this size – especially that

56

grizzly grey colour – is so boring without something to brighten it."

Charles's eyebrows lifted fractionally.

"And curtains," Aunt Hester went on, warming to her subject, "instead of those grey silk blinds. Tangerine or pink or scarlet."

"This is a sunny room," Charles said patiently. "It cries out for cool treatment."

"Cries out for a woman's touch, more like. It needs cheering up. But there I go forgetting, you two lovebirds will soon be married." There was a touch of acid in her voice despite her smiling glance. "What will you do, Polly? Brighten the place up with pink curtains and cosy rugs?"

"I'll think about it when the time comes," she said easily, applying herself to the plate of spicy grilled chicken and tender broccoli: she was always deeply appreciative of Mrs Sheppard's cooking. She let the discussion – argument – flow unheeded about her.

The two people she loved most dearly – her mother's sister and her father's boyhood friend – seemed destined to strike sparks off one other whenever they met. They probably enjoyed it in a funny sort of way. Individually, Hester and Charles had qualities that Polly admired and respected. Put them together and they brought out the worst in each other.

Yet whatever their differences, they were united in having her interests at heart. Between them they had provided the necessary balance and security which a shocked and terrified orphan had so badly needed. Aunt Hester had given her unstinted warmth and comfort. Charles, practical and cautious, had dealt with all the legal and financial aspects of her parents' estate. She'd been placed in a small boarding school for the year her parents had been abroad and, thanks to Charles's care of her finances, she was able to continue her education there. It was only later that she understood exactly what that stability had meant to her and how much both these dear people had done to protect and cosset her. One or other – or both – would appear at school events, take her out for treats, organise her holidays; and never for one moment had she been made to feel any kind of burden, or an inconvenient responsibility. It was only later that she wondered how much the two had contributed financially. By the time she was eighteen and able to take control of her own affairs she had expected very little to be left of her inheritance. To her surprise there was a comfortable nest egg. Even if she'd chosen to fritter away her spare time, it would have cushioned her comfortably through the year she spent learning the basics of her profession at college. But she'd worked hard, taking on weekend and evening jobs, so as to preserve what she could of her money. Not only did she have the ambition to do well in the career she'd chosen, but she possessed a fierce determination to make them both proud of her: to repay them in the best way she knew, by showing that their faith in her was justified.

It had been tough, but slowly all the hard work and dedication was beginning to pay off.

Looking at them now, as they gently bickered across the ebony and white expanse of the table, she knew how grateful she was to them both and how much she loved these two such different people.

Hester, with her exuberant red hair and her be-ringed fingers, brought a touch of drama to the quiet room. Charles looked calm and at ease, his finely drawn features, carefully groomed grey hair, dark business suit and immaculate white shirt complementing the restrained decor. Almost, she thought with amusement, as though he'd designed himself into it, which, in a way, perhaps he had. Or rather the house had taken on his personal style, and into this habitat he fitted as naturally as a hand into a comfortable glove.

By the time they were sitting over coffee in the square black leather armchairs of the drawing room, Hester and Charles were needling each other over the merits of the current London shows and Polly was remembering how she had broken the news of her engagement to her aunt. She had expected fireworks. She had got a stunned silence.

"It was when we were together so much, collaborating over the book," Polly said carefully. "We realised we wanted to go on seeing more of each other. Then Charles – we – decided to put things on a more permanent basis."

Hester's eyes were wide. After a moment she said, her voice husky, "Are you sure about this, Polly?"

"If it's the age difference that's bothering you—"

"Age doesn't come into it," Hester said sharply. "Some people are middle-aged at twenty. I've known seventy-year-olds with the outlook of teenagers. But Charles . . ."

"We're perfectly compatible. You know we've always got on well."

"As friends, yes. As a father figure, yes. But as marriage partners? As lovers?"

"I'm not a child! I'm twenty-five. I've built up my own business. And Charles is not my father! I don't see him that way at all."

"Polly, you've lived like a nun."

"How can you possibly know that?" Despite the betraying heat that flared in her cheeks, she held on to her indignation. "I had boyfriends enough at college," she said. But after one brief and disastrous encounter when she was eighteen, she had refused to allow any relationship to develop beyond a few chaste dates. The experience had been a complete turn-off. Her own fault for being so stupid, as much as the boy's. He was head-swivellingly handsome and popular. She'd been dazzled, flattered, even envied when his attention lighted on her for that few hours at a party. It was only later she discovered what a shallow, self-centred creep he was. Out of shyness among people who were still strangers, out of a need to feel part of the noisy crowd, she'd downed too much of the cheap red wine. Her judgement, the fear even that might have kept her aware and cautious, were eroded by the numbing, blurring effects of the alcohol. She remembered lying down, eyes tightly shut, and the world spinning and spinning . . . She felt remote, disembodied, as though the drunken scrabbling on the bed was happening to someone else. When it was over he'd left with scarcely a word. On to his next conquest. The next scalp to hang on his belt. Next day's agonising hangover she'd accepted as rightful punishment for her stupidity. She'd felt soiled and used, and on some deep level shamed and scared. She hated the feeling, justified or not, that she was the subject of sniggering among his cronies. After that she kept aloof. And sober. Better to concentrate on important things without distraction. There'd be plenty of time for all that later.

"And since?" asked Hester.

"You know very well I've been far too busy with the business. Besides," she added huffily, "since when did sleeping around automatically qualify you for marriage?"

Hester sighed. "I didn't mean that at all." She reached out and touched Polly's hand. "I don't want to spoil things for you. I'm sure Charles will do his best to make you happy. He's a kind man. Not my type, of course – but is he yours?" She shook her head. "It's just that I wonder if you really understand yourself."

Polly laughed. "Oh, come on."

"There's something – I don't know – an unawakened quality about you." The green eyes were unexpectedly troubled. "Yes, you can laugh and I suppose I am being silly, but I do feel you're making a mistake. Charles isn't the man to make you truly happy."

"But he is! Honestly, Aunt Hes, I'm not going into this with blinkers on. We'll be fine."

"You may be a whizz with a camera, but I doubt if your judgement's too sound in other areas. You should get about more, play the field a bit, before you tie yourself to a man twenty years older and set in his ways."

"That's your opinion. I have mine."

"And what about the photography? This important career of yours."

"What about it?" Polly was genuinely surprised. "You don't for a minute suppose Charles is going to start playing the heavy Victorian husband. Not even you could believe that of him."

"No. No of course not." Hester shook her head, then managed a somewhat strained smile that didn't quite reach her eyes. "Forgive me, darling. I shouldn't interfere. You're absolutely right. You're not my little niece any more. You're grown up and perfectly capable of taking grown-up decisions. I wish you both well. I truly do."

"Thanks." Polly gave her aunt a hug. "It'll work, you see. An understanding husband, a satisfying career, what more could I ask?"

What more could I ask? she echoed silently to herself as she sipped the strong coffee in an effort to fight against the tiredness that was starting to overwhelm her. There was really nothing she could think of that would add to the sum total of her contentment at this moment. She was incredibly fortunate.

Aunt Hester departed in a flurry of Dior-scented embraces. Polly waved her off in a taxi for Paddington and the Torquay train and unsuccessfully tried to stifle a yawn as Charles closed the door.

"Time you were heading home," he said with a sympathetic pat on her arm. "Overnight travel's always exhausting."

"That delicious lunch didn't help," she said, eyes watering in an effort to suppress another yawn. "I ate far too much. I always do. Mrs Sheppard cooks like a dream."

"It had to be extra special today," he said quietly. "I've missed you, my dear."

"I missed you, too," she said. "The holiday was great, but it's good to be back."

"I half believed that you might be dazzled by the attentions of some . . . new admirer while you were away." The hesitation was fractional. She knew he'd just avoided saying 'younger'. It was something he was sensitive about, something she never gave a thought to.

She kissed his cheek lightly. "Like that awful Leon Hammond, you mean? No thanks."

"Awful, was he? I thought he seemed rather agreeable."

"Too pushy for my taste."

"Hester seemed to be getting on well with him."

"She's a born flirt."

Charles shook his head, smiling. "And she never did have any discrimination. Or taste."

Another yawn loomed. "Sorry," Polly said. "I'm whacked. Despite flying in relative comfort, I can't say I slept much. Mind you, I could get used to travelling in superior style."

"I'd run you home," Charles said, looking a little edgy as he eyed his watch, "but I have this appointment. I've already put it on hold once . . ."

"Taxi'll be fine," she said sleepily.

"I'm afraid I'm rather tied up the next few days, too."

"Not to worry. I'll have a mountain of work to catch up with myself," she said, trying to remember where she'd dropped her bag. Then she spotted it by her chair in the drawing room.

It looked a bit sad lying there, its shabbiness emphasised by the smooth black leather of the chair. It was a large, brown, squashy leather bag with an infinity of useful pockets, but it was showing its age and the shoulder strap was looking very worn. A pity. She was very fond of it. But she'd have to think of a replacement. And that, unfortunately, meant shopping. Yuck.

Charles was casting ever more urgent glances at his watch. "We'll meet up on Saturday then. I'll book a table at *Mario's* and pick you up about seven. Oh, and the Scotts have asked us over for drinks and lunch on Sunday."

Polly heaved a contented sigh. *Mario's*, the Scotts, the backlog of work waiting for her at home . . . Her life was slipping back into its usual safe pattern. Safe? Satisfying, she meant. Of course she did.

"I'll look forward to it," she said, as he kissed her goodbye.

The strap on Polly's bag snapped on Friday afternoon as she yanked it off the back of her office chair to rummage in its voluminous depths for a mislaid business card on which she'd jotted an appointment time.

"Blast! I'll really have to brace myself now and face the shops," she grumbled to Kate as she vainly tried to staple the frayed ends of the strap together. "I suppose I do need a couple of new shirts, as well. I had the iron too hot when I was pressing the white one last night. I meant to wear it on Sunday. Might as well do the lot in one fell swoop . . . Ouch!" The staple jabbed into her thumb as the leather tore again. She gave up her attempts at resuscitation. "I'll have to go tomorrow."

"Not before time," Kate said, busy filing sheets of transparencies. "Make my day. Buy something with a bit of street cred."

"Not you as well. I have enough with Aunt Hes. Well, I can't face bloody Oxford Street on a Saturday. I'll see if I can get fixed up locally."

Kate groaned. "There's nothing halfway decent round here. Look, you need help. Why don't you let me—"

"Oh, no, no, no!" Polly held up her hands. "We've quite enough with one peacock in the office, thank you."

"Me?" Kate looked down at herself. "I just like to give the place a bit of pzazz."

"Pzazz? If I turned up in orange dungarees and a scarlet sweater with a whole jeweller's window dangling from my ears, my clients would turn tail and flee."

"Bollocks. They'd be impressed. They'd mark you

down as arty and creative, instead of some kind of mousey office nerd."

Polly took no notice. Most of the time she thanked heaven that she'd taken Kate on. In eighteen months, since she'd been able to afford help, Kate had become indispensable. Only occasionally and briefly, like now, did she wish she had employed someone a bit less brash and outspoken.

Something about Kate had appealed to Polly from the first. After a succession of well-qualified, beautifully-groomed applicants, it had seemed madness to pick an urchin like Kate. She had bounced into the interview like a violently coloured kitten clutching a handful of barely-dry diplomas and proceeded to talk herself into the job. Polly had found herself almost mesmerised into giving her a trial. Perhaps it was the flicker of shrewd intelligence in her brown eyes, the good humour evident behind the brashness. Whatever it was, Polly had not regretted employing her. Now, she ran the office, the computer and Polly with cheerful efficiency. And, eager to add to her skills, she'd turned out to be no mean darkroom assistant to boot.

"So what are you planning to buy? A nice boring frock to make you invisible at Christmas parties?"

"I don't want to even think about Christmas yet. Too much to do."

"And what about this visit to the lady of the manor next week?"

"What's wrong with my suit?"

"God, it's gross."

"Plenty of wear in it yet," Polly said cheerfully. "Anyway, I hate shopping for clothes. Such a waste of time."

Kate grabbed the book and wagged it under Polly's

nose. "You're forgetting you've a reputation now to live up to. That shapeless black thing you're so fond of makes you look like an undertaker's assistant instead of a successful photographer." She dropped the book on the desk and stomped back to the light box. "Do it! Make an impression! Get yourself noticed!"

Polly looked at the bold book jacket with its eye-catching colours. She was torn between pleasure and unease at what the critics had said. Kate had clipped and filed all the reviews from the newspapers, the glossies and the relevant professional magazines. Without exception they had waxed lyrical about the photographs, but she hoped Charles wasn't going to be too upset by the acid comments about his writing style.

'*Amateurish and long winded,*' – Leon Hammond had said. It gave her no pleasure to have his opinion confirmed, but she wasn't going to think about *him*.

Polly found the missing card and jotted the name and time in her diary. The pages looked satisfactorily full. The photographs in *Follies* had caused a flutter of interest in several quarters. A local radio station had already recorded an interview with her to be slotted into their next arts programme. A gallery in Oxford had asked to see some of her work with a view to including it in an exhibition of young talent. There'd been quite a few other enquiries with interesting possibilities. Perhaps the most intriguing was from a woman who lived in Dorset. She'd been so impressed with the photographs that she'd made an appointment for Polly to go and look over her manor house. It was of historic and architectural interest, she'd told Kate, and she was thinking of commissioning a full portfolio of professional photographs as a record for the family.

Kate had made all the arrangements for Polly's preliminary visit and Mrs Helen Carpenter had suggested she should stay overnight at the manor. "She's really keen that you get the feel of the place," Kate had told her. "And before you ask, I checked in Pevsner. The house is big on plasterwork, apparently, some nice windows and the Victorians pretty well left it alone."

Which sounded more than promising.

Kate spread another batch of transparencies on to the light box. "A horsey, tweedy sort of place, d'you think? Or a posh retreat for some wealthy city type with Helen wotsit dripping designer labels. Better be prepared, Poll."

"I'm there to work, not swan around in a Chanel frock. Which reminds me, I must pack my wellies. The countryside'll probably be awash after all this rain."

"You'll be eating there. They might go for the dressing for dinner sort of stuff."

"I'm probably ranked as the hired help. I might be consigned to eat with the serfs in the kitchen."

"Or you could be scoffing off gold plate in the baronial hall. You need something halfway decent, just in case. And don't mention the black suit if you value your life."

"Something to go with suits of armour and howling draughts, then? Chain mail, perhaps?"

"Yeah, kinky. However, I've got this friend . . ."

Polly groaned. Kate had a whole network of friends and relations involved in enterprises of one kind or another who were always able to offer hefty discounts or cheap end-of-ranges.

"She's in the rag trade," Kate went on unabashed. "Got her own little business."

"Is it legal?" asked Polly suspiciously.

Kate turned to look at her with an expression of affronted innocence. "Naturally."

"What's natural about it? Some of your connections seem dangerously connected to the backs of lorries and things falling off same."

"Not Janey," Kate said, in shocked tones. "She's a product of St Martin's, no less."

"And what's that got to do with the price of eggs?"

"She's brilliant. She could design you something that'll knock your eye out."

"Very gory. But designer prices are out."

"She does ready-to-wear. I'm sure if I asked—"

"Thanks, but no thanks."

"And on the way to Janey's, we almost pass the shop where my Auntie works."

"We?"

"Boutiquey sort of place. Cheap and cheerful but tons of style."

"No."

"With their expertise and my eye for fashion—"

"*Your* eye?"

Kate grinned. "You don't want to go yomping round shops all by yourself, do you now? Not when I've got a free day. Not when I've got these mates who'll fix you up a treat. No hassle. No pain."

"You promise?"

"Trust me."

"As if I would."

Polly gave in. If she was honest, the prospect of being towed round by Kate was far more appealing than a solitary mooch. It would be good for a laugh if nothing else, and if she couldn't see anything suitable there was still the despised black suit.

"Give it to the Sally Army," Kate said as they sat over a late lunchtime snack in a crowded cafe on Saturday. "It's just right to keep some poor old bag-lady decent."

"It's not that bad," Polly protested, sipping a restorative coffee.

"It is" Kate said.

Polly's feet ached and her clothes had been on and off so many times she felt battered. And not only physically. She and Kate seemed to have been locked in battle all morning. But it was done. She'd bought far too much, spent far too much. It was shocking quite how much she had been manoeuvred into spending. But she'd worry about that when the credit card bill came in. And it was all over and done with, thank heaven. For a good long time, she hoped.

Kate looked thoroughly complacent, as she eyed the heap of plastic bags. "I was right wasn't I? You just needed the right person to bully you into getting some decent clobber."

"Bully being the operative word."

"Had to. You argued every inch of the way. Even though you hadn't a clue what you were talking about." Kate sank her small white teeth into a huge cream cake. "Charles'll go bananas with lust when he sees you in that green number."

Polly frowned. "I shouldn't have let you and Janey bulldoze me into buying that. The other stuff will be okay, I suppose. But that green thing just isn't me."

"It's you all right," Kate said. "Even those bits of you that aren't usually on display."

Polly eyed her over the rim of her coffee cup. "Those bits are far better covered up in my opinion," she said.

Anne Goring

"Shut up and eat your sandwich. Auntie Kate knows best. Believe it."

Polly didn't. As she dressed to go to *Mario's* that evening, she viewed the green dress with dismay, what little there was of it. She hastily pushed it to the back of the wardrobe. But at least the other gear was more wearable, this outfit for one. Sort of coffee colour jersey skirt and top, and a long jacket with cream trim. "That'll take you anywhere," Kate had insisted. "Plain T-shirt under the jacket for visiting clients, dressed up with a silk shirt for evening. Then there's the slacks . . . you should get those. And this other darker skirt to go with the jacket. Different style, different effect. I told you Janey was clever, didn't I?"

Polly had actually been quite impressed. Janey had an unexpectedly subtle collection, all soft colours and flowing, easy-to-wear shapes. It all looked quite ordinary and inoffensive on the hangers, but once she put them on she'd been surprised how different they made her look. Too different, she'd thought, suspiciously at first. But in the end, tired of arguing, she'd given in. At least the green dress was the only desperate mistake. The rest was pretty wearable. Kate had cheerfully assured her they were dirt cheap for the quality. Polly, making a mental total of the price tags, had felt weak at the knees as she visualised the camera gear she could have bought for the money. But at least she needn't shop for another garment for a long, long time and the whole buying spree – including a session in the aunt's boutique choosing accessories – had been accomplished in not much more than half a day.

Polly brushed her hair and tied it back, whizzed a dab of foundation and blusher on her face and a scrape of lip

70

gloss on her mouth. She decided to ignore the mascara and eyeshadow Kate had casually given her as a present. She could never be bothered with much make-up. Waste of time. She heard the Rover pull up outside the house as she went downstairs, grabbing her trench coat from the hook in the tiny hall and thinking as she always did how lucky she'd been to get this place.

When she'd moved to this particular corner of north London three years ago, Charles had been concerned that the district was a bit seedy. But there was no way she could have gone for anything in a better area. As it was she could only just about manage the deposit and mortgage. And she was desperate to get out of her cramped rented flat in Camden. Aunt Hester had been more encouraging. "Mm, I think you might be on to a good thing here, darling. The house is basically sound. Convenient for the Tube. Cul-de-sac, so no traffic rat-runs. End of terrace and with room at the side to make a run-in for the car. Always an advantage when you come to sell."

"Whoa! I haven't even said I'll take it."

"Well, my feeling, for what it's worth, is that you could do worse. These Victorian artisans' cottages, once they're done up, can look pretty good."

The house did look pretty good now. Her first priority had been a darkroom, studio and office downstairs. The tiny galley kitchen extension had been added by a previous owner at the back. Upstairs, the two original bedrooms were now a bedroom and sitting room. Just before Aunt Hester had whisked her off to Africa, she'd had a new ivory bathroom suite put in to replace the manure-coloured 1960s monstrosity she'd inherited.

When the Christmas rush was over, she planned to set about tiling and painting.

From the beginning she'd resisted all offers of money – gifts or loans – from Charles or her aunt. This was her baby, her career, and she was determined to make it on her own terms and in her own way.

It had been tough at first but she'd been willing to take on any sort of routine work in order to keep going – gradually improving her technique, steadily building up the side of the business she most enjoyed. Now everything was coming together. She had a retainer from one architectural consortium and regular work from smaller practices. She was making a respectable profit from the bread-and-butter work – photographing products in her studio for a couple of advertising agencies, most of which she ploughed back in to the business – and her name was becoming known for quality and innovation. By way of a bonus, local property prices had started to rise. Several houses in the street had recently been snapped up and were being improved by young, professional people.

"I think you started a trend," Charles remarked as they drove away past a neighbouring house gleaming with new paint under the street lights. "I can see this street becoming the place to live for the upwardly mobile. You made a good investment. You'll make a handsome profit when the time comes to sell up."

"I suppose so."

"But there's plenty of time to deal with that after we're married."

"After we're . . . ? But I hadn't even thought . . . I mean it's where I work. I've just got everything as I want it."

"I know that, Polly." He took his eyes off the road to smile at her reassuringly. "And I certainly wouldn't want to rush you, or persuade you to do anything against your wishes. But I think it's something you should consider."

"You've been thinking about it, obviously," she said, feeling unaccountably piqued.

"True. But only because I think it would be in your own best interests."

"Why?"

"The commuting for one," he said reasonably. "You work from home now, and you don't need me to tell you how convenient that is. You could have those two spare top-floor rooms in my house, our house, next to my study. It would give me the greatest pleasure to plan the conversion for you. And a new upmarket address wouldn't do your business any harm, would it?"

It was so sensible, so logical and Charles sounded so pleased with the idea. Why then did she feel this quick, instinctive antagonism?

She had a sudden vision of Kate with her outrageous clothes and clanking jewelry invading the minimilist calm of Charles's house. She smiled. "It would mean a lot more travelling time for Kate," she said.

"Oh, Kate." Charles's tone was dismissive. He gestured with his hand as though waving away an irritation. "You'd soon train up another assistant if she doesn't want to move."

"That's scarcely the point," Polly protested. "I care about Kate. We work well together and she's become a friend."

There was a small silence, then Charles said gently. "I'm sorry, my dear. I did put my suggestion a little clumsily. It's just that I want the best for you, that's all.

73

I won't interfere any more. You must decide for yourself exactly what you want and I'll be happy to go along with that. After all, I wouldn't want our reunion evening to get off to a bad start." He smiled. "I've looked forward to it so much."

"Me too."

It was rarely that they argued and usually it was no more than a mild difference of opinion, soon settled. Polly was taken aback by the flash of anger that had, momentarily, been quite powerful.

"Look in the glove compartment," Charles went on. "There's a little homecoming present for you."

After the briefest of hesitations, Polly reached for the small package.

"Go on. Open it."

She slid off the wrapping to reveal a tiny oval silver box engraved with a flowing and intricate design of leaves. "Oh, it's beautiful," she murmured. "What a lovely surprise. Thank you." She leaned across and kissed his cheek.

"'Bid me love, and I will give a loving heart to thee,'" he quoted lightly. "Who wrote that? Herrick?" He cleared his throat and stared at the tail lights of the car ahead. "Whoever it was, I commend the sentiment."

She was touched. He was not a man to whom sentimental words or gestures came easily. Their courtship had been conducted with almost Victorian correctness. Yet he surprised her at unexpected moments with gifts, with poetic quotations, as though only through these little gestures, through the words of other people, he was able to express his own thoughts.

She felt guilty that she had been sharp with him and made a determined effort to be extra pleasant and attentive

74

that evening, even when he went into a blow-by-blow account of a golf match he had won in her absence. She had tried and failed to raise any enthusiasm for the game. She'd confessed as much to Charles, who had laughed and made light of it.

"No matter, my dear," he had said tolerantly. "I can't expect you to share all my interests, though I do hope I may occasionally call upon you to entertain the wives of some of my more important contacts."

"Of course," she had agreed. He did a great deal of PR in an informal way on the golf course. She knew that, though she did hope that she wasn't called upon too often to act as nursemaid to stray, non-golfing wives. She wanted very much for their married life to meld their separate lives into a joint, supportive whole, but she also felt that to be landed for hours at a stretch with some unknown woman with whom she might have nothing in common, might tax her rather frail line in small talk. So far, thankfully, it was a role she hadn't been called upon to play.

She bore the talk of birdies and eagles with good grace that evening. Afterwards he took her home. He had told her frankly from the first that there was no question that he'd ever want to stay the night. He'd smiled and stroked her cheek. "I've got old-fashioned views on marriage," he said. "Crazy, isn't it, in this day and age? Oh, I know I've had women friends – relationships – over the years. But I've been content to drift along, steering clear of any long-term committment. Now it's different. And I want to make that difference clear to myself and to you."

"Why me? Why now?" she'd asked.

"You're special, Polly. I want our marriage to be

75

special. For both of us. As to why now? I'm forty-four. I
have everything I've worked hard for – a solid architectural practice that enables me to live well and comfortably
– but I look ahead, and the future . . . well, let's say I'd
like to be sharing it with someone I hold very dear."

She found his little speech very moving. And he'd been
true to his word. If she was honest, the arrangement suited
her very well. She wanted her marriage to be built on the
secure foundation of kindness and consideration and as
far removed as possible from that seedy and shameful
encounter with the college Lothario. That Charles would
be a considerate lover, she had no doubt. She was quite
prepared to wait.

So he didn't stay long once they'd had a coffee and a
cuddle. It was only after he'd gone that the angry, uncomfortable little feeling she'd had earlier in the evening
returned. Charles wanted her to sell up. He'd left it for
now. Left it up to her, he said. But she knew, sooner or
later, the subject would come up again. And she didn't
want to sell her house, she didn't want that at all.

It was late but she felt too unsettled to go straight to
bed after she'd locked the front door. Instead she went
through the downstairs rooms one by one, switching on
lights, looking round. Then she went upstairs to the small
sitting room. It was nothing special. Not to anyone but
her. A couple of squashy armchairs, bought second-hand
– she'd made the yellow covers herself, and also the
matching curtains drawn across the window against the
darkness outside. A few rugs on floorboards that she'd
scraped and polished until they gleamed like parquet. A
mahogany gateleg table – a junk shop find – that folded
tidily against the wall, but that she could open out if she
invited Kate or Charles or Aunt Hes to supper. Creamy

stippled walls and a couple of pottery lamps with gold lampshades casting a warm glow. Family photographs, a few well-loved prints and a couple of blow-ups of special photographs of her own covered the walls. She wandered into the bedroom. She'd done this room up in apricot and cream, splashing out on a fitted carpet and a duvet cover with a lacy edge.

Charles had told her, kindly, that she'd created a pleasant atmosphere. It was true. It was comfortable, homely. The rooms had a warm, welcoming atmosphere. To her, whenever she walked in, she could almost hear herself being bidden to kick off her shoes, pick up a book and relax.

She undressed slowly and went to bed. But she couldn't sleep. She stared wide-eyed into the darkness, her thoughts coasting backwards down the years to her childhood.

Her parents had led peripatetic lives, moving about the country from one rented house to another. Her young life had been full of change. Each year it seemed there was a new house, new school, new friends to make. It hadn't always been easy. Sometimes she felt she was skimming along the edge of things, the outsider, never given a chance to settle to permanent friendships before it was up sticks and off somewhere else. She had learned self-sufficiency early, learned not to care too much when she was shut out of playground intrigues, learned not to get too deeply attached to any one place or any one person. The constant in her life was the love that surrounded her at home. Where that home happened to be didn't matter. Even the year she was to spend at boarding school in Somerset when she was eight while her parents worked in the dusty heat and political uncertainty of a country that teetered on the brink of internecine war hadn't seemed too much of a trial. There were the regular letters and phone calls, the excitement of the visits in the school holidays. Until that last time . . .

Abruptly, she wrenched her thoughts away, forcing her mind to leap ahead to the years when the comfortable little school, with its dedicated and understanding staff, had given her stability when she most needed it. In those years she had spent her holidays with Aunt Hester at her flat in Torquay or in a cottage she rented in southern France and, in her teens, she visited Charles in London so that he could take her to museums and exhibitions and concerts. Once she was at college it was dingy student digs. Afterwards, it had been a succession of cheap bedsits. Always other people's houses.

This was the first home she could truly call hers. Her refuge for three busy, satisfying years. With a sense of dismay, she realised she didn't want to give it up. She didn't want to sell.

Or move into Charles' immaculate, well-ordered house?

Her mind sidestepped the question; she didn't want to answer it now. It had been a hectic week – the long flight home, the backlog of work – and she'd eaten too much rich food at *Mario's*, drunk too much excellent wine. She was in no state to think logically and clearly. Time enough tomorrow. All she did know was that Charles's assumption that she would sell her house had taken her by surprise. Once she'd had time to consider it properly, she wouldn't be so touchy when he raised the matter again . . .

But Charles didn't mention it at all when they went to lunch with the Scotts at Marlow. He seemed preoccupied, quiet, a little pale.

"Didn't sleep too well," he admitted as they drove north up the M40 towards Buckinghamshire. "Throat's a bit scratchy. Cold coming on, I think."

"Perhaps a breath of country air will clear your head," she said.

"It's certainly a glorious morning."

"A perfect December day," she agreed. "Hope we have time for a walk by the river."

Marlow drowsed in Sunday idleness along the curves of the Thames, frost-tinged water-meadows and chalky hills crowned with stands of beeches that had spread rich golden carpets of fallen leaves along the road verges.

Tom – an old friend of Charles – and Vera Scott welcomed them warmly into the large red-brick house Charles had designed for them in half an acre of abandoned orchard. There were several middle-aged couples there, professional people like Tom and Vera who were doctors. Polly spotted several familiar faces from previous visits. She moved quietly among them, smiling, chatting, sipping a generous glass of sherry that Tom had pressed into her hand.

The day drifted on in a calm, unhurried fashion. After the hot buffet lunch someone half-heartedly suggested a walk. Polly looked up to agree, but held back when the general consensus was that it was far too comfortable indoors. She glanced encouragingly at Charles, but Vera had just given him a couple of paracetamol and he was hunched by the fire hugging a glass of hot lemon.

"Sorry, Polly," he said. "I'm really not up to doing much at all. In fact I think we'd better leave early."

"Lot of flu about," Tom said cheerfully. "Had your jabs, Charles?"

He nodded. "After last winter my doctor thought it for

the best, but I hope this is just a cold." He sneezed by way of emphasis.

Polly's disappointment that they weren't going to take advantage of such a glorious afternoon was instantly tempered by concern. Charles had only picked at the delicious lunch and he was looking decidedly under the weather. She was reminded that last winter he'd had a nasty virus that had turned to pneumonia and landed him in hospital. She hoped he wasn't sickening for anything like that again.

"I expect it's nothing a good night's sleep won't put right," Tom said, his eyes twinkling in his good-natured, bluff-featured face. "I bet you've been overdoing it, eh? Living it up with young Polly here, I dare say, since she's returned from the fleshpots."

"Not at all," said Charles, somewhat coolly.

"You mustn't forget that you're not twenty-five any more." Tom guffawed, oblivious of the quick frown that drew Charles's brows together.

"If you don't mind Tom, I think it might be best if we got on our way," Polly put in quickly, knowing how sensitive Charles was about having the difference in their ages pointed up. She smiled, adding lightly, "Nowhere like home when you're feeling rough. And an early night won't do Charles any harm."

"Polly, my love, you're absolutely spot on," Tom said. "You drive him home, tuck him up in his bachelor bed and make sure he calls his GP if he's no better tomorrow."

"Polly has far better things to do than fuss over me," Charles said stiffly.

"I wouldn't say that." Tom winked at her. "You've got a vested interest, haven't you, in seeing Charlie here makes it to the altar? Have you named the day yet? You want to pin him down, Polly, before he slips the noose."

"Sometimes Tom is a bit overpowering," Charles said as he backed the Rover out of the drive. He'd refused to let Polly drive, insisting that he was perfectly capable. Almost, thought Polly, as if he'd taken Tom's remarks as a challenge. "Still, perhaps he's right in one respect. We should be setting the date for our wedding."

He inched the car down the narrow lane and out on to the main road. Polly stared through the windscreen at the shivery grey wraiths of mist gathering over the darkening fields, hazing the headlights of the oncoming cars.

"Yes, I suppose we should," she said softly.

"Did I tell you I'd been offered a villa in the Algarve?"

"No."

"The conversion on that Essex barn I was telling you about. I was out there while you were away, as planning permission's gone through. Anyway, the owner's a very pleasant chap. He has this villa he lends to friends when he's not using it himself. He was very keen to let me have it. It's free in April, apparently. If we married at Easter we could honeymoon there."

"Portugal. Have you been there, Charles?"

"A couple of times. I know the area from a couple of golfing holidays. The villa's in a small village not too far from the coast, but well away from the crowds. Some very good restaurants. Excellent golf course there. What do you think?"

"Mm. Sounds . . . possible."

"I have to say it sounds ideal to me. The villa comes with maid service, and at that time of year the weather would be pleasant. Not too hot and uncomfortable." He glanced at her, eyebrows raised. "What do you think?"

"Depends," she said cautiously. "What's it like? I mean, we want to be sure it's okay."

He smiled. "Now you know me, Polly. I wouldn't commit us to anything without a thorough investigation. I've seen photographs, of course, and just to be on the safe side I contacted a mutual acquaintance who's actually stayed with his family in the villa. He gave me a very favourable report."

"Well, I suppose we could think about it." She didn't know why she couldn't muster more enthusiasm. Perhaps it was the mention of golf. But it was hardly likely Charles would want to take his golf clubs on honeymoon, was it? Surely not. No, it couldn't be that. More likely she'd harboured vague notions of being swept off to some romantic, tropical isle. All sugar-white beaches, frangipani blossom and moonlit, barefoot walks under the stars. And mosquitoes and sand flies, she reminded herself sharply. Paradise always had a down side. Portugal would be perfectly pleasant, but still . . . "How long do we have before we decide?"

"I said I'd let him know by Christmas."

Time enough to get used to the idea. To be pleased about it, as Charles evidently was. And by Christmas, with their wedding in prospect, she'd be perfectly reconciled to selling her house. Everything would slot into place nicely. Of course it would. By then, she'd probably look back and wonder why she'd ever felt this niggling sense of unease.

Perhaps it was to do with the night beyond their warm cocoon of metal and glass. They were on the motorway now and the fog loomed up at them in dense, blinding patches. There was always something melancholy about a foggy landscape at the tail-end of the year, as though the wraiths of mist personified the sad, dying spirit of the season. By day, fog and mist could give magical effects to photographs. It was a bonus she appreciated if she was on a shoot. Not tonight, however. Despite the heater on full blast because Charles was feeling shivery, she wasn't overwarm herself: the fog seemed to reach in to cast its louring chill into her mind.

Pure imagination!

"I'll put a tape on, shall I?" she said brightly, opening the cassette holder. "What would you like? Something cheerful . . . let's see."

"If you don't mind, my dear," Charles said, "I'd prefer not to have the distraction. Not in these conditions. I need all my concentration and I've quite a headache, anyway."

"Oh, sorry."

Deflated, she replaced the tapes and sat back. Then, as Charles seemed disinclined to talk, she closed her eyes against the night and turned her mind resolutely to mulling over all she had to do in the week ahead.

She spent the whole of Monday in the darkroom, emerging for a quick snack at lunchtime at Kate's insistence, and finalising the last batch of black and white prints long after Kate had gone home. She left the prints washing and, somewhat guiltily, went to ring Charles. Poor love, he'd been looking quite white and exhausted by the time he'd dropped her off last evening. The drive home in the fog hadn't helped, with conditions getting steadily more difficult. She'd fully intended to phone earlier to make sure he was okay, but somehow the hours had slipped away without her noticing – not an uncommon occurrence when she was absorbed in her work. The feeling of guilt intensified when he answered the phone. His voice was no more than a husky whisper, he was already in bed. The cold, it seemed, had worsened considerably.

"Would you like me to come over?" she asked anxiously. "Is there anything I can get you?"

"Nothing," he croaked. "And no point in coming over at this time of night."

"It's not eight yet. I don't like to think of you on your own."

"Mrs Sheppard's only just gone. She will fuss, because I'd been to the office and she thought I should have stayed at home. She made me come up to bed early. I'd just dozed off when you rang."

"Oh, dear. Sorry. Tomorrow, then."

"I might work at home tomorrow," he said.

"Sensible. It's a filthy weather forecast. Cold and wet. If you like, I'll nip over at lunchtime. How does that sound?"

"Are you sure? Wouldn't want you to get my germs," he said morosely. "You're off to Dorset on Wednesday, aren't you? You want to be feeling your best, not more dead than alive."

"Blow the germs. I can't possibly go without seeing you," she protested. "Expect me about one, bearing lots of invalid comforts."

She kept the rest of the brief conversation light and cheerful, and he did sound marginally brighter by the time she hung up.

"You're a very sweet girl," he managed towards the end. "And I make a poor invalid, Polly. So do forgive me for being a touch grouchy."

"I'd be pretty grouchy in your shoes. Or should it be bedsocks? No, ignore that. Just you have a good night's sleep and I'll see you tomorrow. Love you."

She arrived on Charles's doorstep in driving, sleety rain, armed with black grapes, half a dozen of the sweet Florida grapefruit that he particularly liked and a box of his favourite chocolates. Mrs Sheppard ushered her in, looking worried, and Polly was taken aback to see a middle-aged woman, crisply uniformed in white, hovering in the hall behind her. A nurse! Polly stared at her in alarm.

"Charles . . . Mr Gregson? What's happened?"

"Mr Gregson is quite comfortable." The nurse's tone was as crisp and impersonal as her uniform.

"Polly, love, I told him he shouldn't have gone to the office yesterday." Mrs Sheppard was clearly upset. "I called the doctor first thing, as soon as I came in. Poor Mr G's got full-blown bronchitis."

"Everything is quite under control," the nurse said. She had a smooth plump face and pale blue eyes that she turned somewhat coolly on Mrs Sheppard. "Mr Gregson is resting now. If it's convenient, I should very much like that cup of tea you so kindly offered me earlier."

Mrs Sheppared hurried off. The pale blue gaze returned enquiringly to Polly.

"Do I take it that you are Miss Burton, Mr Gregson's fiancée? I see. Mrs Sheppard told me you were expected." She held out a smooth plump hand. "Megan Lacey. Sister Lacey. Such a shock for you, I'm sure."

"So how bad is he?" Polly took the hand offered to her, feeling her own to be less than hygenic against the scrubbed pink fingers.

"Doctor Roberts thought it best, as a purely precautionary measure, if Mr Gregson had professional attention for a few days. Just to be on the safe side."

"I'm supposed to be going to Dorset tomorrow," Polly said. "A business trip. Should I cancel, d'you think?"

"I shouldn't think that necessary at all." She raised fine, fair eyebrows. "I do assure you that Doctor Roberts trusts me implicitly where the welfare of his patients is concerned."

"Of course. I didn't mean . . . I wasn't implying . . ."

"I'm sure you weren't"

"But Charles. If he's so poorly . . ."

"He's not in any danger. A few days careful nursing and I'll have him back on his feet. As I explained, this is just a precautionary measure."

"Well, I won't stay long, or tire him or anything." Polly felt young and awkward under that cool, superior gaze. She held up the plastic carrier. "I picked up a few goodies for him. Just fruit and chocolates."

"I'm sure he'll appreciate them in a day or two."

"I'll go up then," Polly said, stepping forward, then stopping when the nurse made no move from where she had stationed herself to block the way to the stairs.

"Mr Gregson, as you may have heard me say, is resting," Sister Lacy said, enunciating slowly and clearly as if Polly were a foreigner who might have some difficulty understanding English spoken at normal speed. "I am hopeful that he might now have fallen asleep. It would be best, in my professional judgement, Miss Burton, if you did not disturb him." She held out her hand for the carrier. "I'll take that for you."

Polly stared at her. The patronising old bat!

"Thanks, but I'd prefer to take it myself," she said, adding by way of explanation and immediately cross with herself for trying to placate the wretched woman. "I know my fiancé would be quite devastated if he knew I hadn't at least looked in on him while I'm here. And don't worry, I promise I'll be very quiet and I won't wake him if he's asleep."

Polly refused to let her glance drop. After a moment, the nurse stood aside. "Very well," she said coldly.

Polly felt the pale blue gaze boring into her back as she ran lightly up the stairs. And it was no consolation that the old dragon was right. Charles was asleep, propped up against a mound of snowy pillows. The curtains were drawn and the rasp of his breathing sounded loud in the dimness. She tiptoed across to the bed and put the fruit and chocolates where he'd see them when he woke. Then she crept out of the room again and pulled the door to quietly behind her.

Sister Lacey's 'I told you so' smirk followed her out into the driving rain.

Polly phoned again before she left for Dorset the next morning. Megan Lacey's superior voice assured her that Mr Gregson had had a comfortable night.

"You run along to Dorset," she said as though Polly were a small child fretting about missing a treat. "And do try not to worry. Doctor Roberts is satisfied that our patient is maintaining the expected progress."

Polly put down the phone with an uncharacteristic slam. "That woman is a—"

"Watch it!" Kate poked her face round the darkroom door. She tapped a finger at the purple dial of the watch that weighed down her skinny wrist. "Never mind slagging off the Lady with the Lamp. You should have left an hour ago while the sun was still out. It's a lousy forecast, you know. This rain is supposed to be turning to snow later on."

Polly groaned. "That's all I need."

"These'll brighten your day," Kate said, handing Polly a packet. "I came in early and ran off a few prints from your African transparencies. No, don't waste time looking at them now. Save them for when you're tucked up in the baronial four-poster. Take your mind off the ghosts queueing up to clank round your bedroom. Now, git!"

Polly aimed a friendly cuff at Kate's head – scarlet streaks in her brown hair today, emerald-green sweater, purple skirt and half a ton of bright yellow beads dangling round her neck and clinking round her wrists. Kate was a whole colour exercise in her own right.

The rain was lashing down as she headed out of London in her old VW. The conditions on the M4 were miserable, with muddy spray flung up from every car and lorry. She was glad when she could cut off on to the Salisbury road, where big flakes of snow began to mix with the rain. She'd been cruising along to the peaceful strains of Kiri Te Kanawa's mellifluous voice and *Songs of the Auvergne*, but as a layer of slush began to settle on the road, she switched off the tape in favour of local radio where, between bursts of pop, there were regular announcements about the traffic and weather conditions.

She could already see the deterioration for herself. The tops of the Wiltshire Downs were already white against the heavy, bruised-looking sky. Dark swirls of snow blew against the windscreen. A couple of times she saw gritting lorries in action, but they didn't seem to be making much impression: snow was already settling on the verges and inching out into the road.

By the time she got to Dorchester her shoulders were aching with tension. She'd planned to stop and stretch her legs, but decided against it. There was, she realised with alarm, a real possibility that she might get stranded. Though the roads through Dorchester town were still passable, the radio was crackling with announcements about minor roads becoming hazardous and the resulting accidents. Not many miles to go, to be sure, but it was all country lanes from now on. She checked the signposts and made up her mind. She reckoned that with luck she'd just about make it.

Dorset was a county she'd always loved. She felt it had an air of ancient mystery, with its softly rounded hills, secret valleys and the marks of ancient settlements and burial mounds patterning fields and slopes. But she was in no mood for romantic imaginings today. Trying to keep in top gear for grip while negotiating the hazardous bends in the narrow lanes took all her concentration. Relief, when she reached the scatter of houses that was the village of Old Radbourne, turned quickly back to anxiety when the turning to the manor proved to be a steep, narrow, high-banked lane where the snow was funnelling down and had already settled inches thick on the road surface.

But she made it. There were the gateposts looming up in the murk, the wrought-iron gates standing open. She pulled thankfully into the curving drive that skirted a shrubbery and opened out into a turning area in front of the manor itself. She stopped the car and cut the engine. In the blessed silence she let out a long relieved sigh. Thank heaven. She peered out at the house and the euphoria of having beaten the snow intensified. At the back of her mind she'd been wondering if the ghastly journey would be worth it. Now she saw that it was. Mellow stone, mullioned windows, gables, the one tall chimney visible from this angle emitting a friendly plume of smoke. Even at first glance she could see the quality of the house.

And someone had noticed her arrival.

The front door had opened and a woman stood there, smiling and waving.

Polly got stiffly out of the car and crunched her way across the snow to the flight of deep stone steps.

"Polly Burton? Hi. Helen Carpenter. Do come along in. I've been half expecting a call to say you'd abandoned the idea of driving down. You poor thing. Has it been a ghastly drive?"

"Another half-hour and I certainly don't think I'd have got through. It's turning into a real blizzard," Polly said, stamping the snow off her shoes and following Helen Carpenter inside.

She was younger than Polly had expected. Thirtyish, fair-haired. No sign of horsey country tweeds or designer country wear. She was wearing jeans and an ordinary pink sweatshirt.

"Don't worry about the car and your luggage," she said cheerfuly. "We'll sort that out in a minute."

The heavy oak door closed on the grey afternoon and Polly was in another world. She had a swift impression of gleaming wood panelling, the fragrance of woodsmoke, the soft glow of lamps as Helen Carpenter ushered her across the wide hall with its gently curving staircase leading to a dimly lit gallery. Then she was in a small sitting room where a log fire crackled in a wide hearth, books and magazines lay scattered comfortably on tables and fat armchairs, and an old black labrador thumped its tail in greeting as it scrambled to its feet and padded across to her.

She bent to pat the dog, only then aware that there was

someone else in the room: a man, who slowly uncoiled himself from where he'd been hidden in the depths of one of the chairs by the hearth.

She looked up, her smile suddenly frozen. Shock took her breath away, held her rigid. She couldn't speak. Her mind refused to acknowledge who it was she was looking at.

He walked across to her – tall, overpoweringly masculine, deep blue eyes glinting with amusement.

"Welcome to Old Radbourne Manor, Polly," Leon Hammond said.

Four

She couldn't move. Her feet were rooted to the carpet.

"What are you doing here?" she managed, eventually, as he advanced towards her.

"Why shouldn't I be?" he said, smiling. "This is my house."

"What?" She looked round at Helen Carpenter. "But you . . ."

"You two know each other?" Helen Carpenter said, sounding puzzled.

"We've met." Polly said grimly.

Helen looked from Polly's shocked face to Leon's amused one. "What's going on, Leon? Getting me to make the arrangements. I thought it was one of your 'I hate publicity' things. What are you up to?"

"Me?" he said innocently. "Just wanted to get one of the best young photographers in the business to photograph my house with the minimum of fuss."

"Don't flannel me," Helen said, bunching her fist and punching his arm in exasperation. "I know that look. You've been getting me into scrapes since I was five years old. There's more to this than meets the eye."

He shook his head. "It's quite simple. If I'd asked

Polly myself, it's quite likely she'd have refused the commission."

"Is that true?" Helen turned to Polly, looking puzzled.

Deep down she wanted to turn and run. But where to in this weather? She doubted she'd even get back up that hill to the village. And though she hated the thought of Leon Hammond pulling such a filthy, underhand trick, this Helen person was clearly as gobsmacked as she was herself. She swallowed, pulled herself together. This was business after all. She'd look a complete idiot if she made a fuss. Nor did she wish to give him the satisfaction of seeing her unnerved. By God, if he wanted photographs of his house, she'd do it. And charge him through the nose for the pleasure of it.

"It's a pity Mr Hammond had to make such a drama out of inviting me here," she said pleasantly. "It was all quite unnecessary. Yes, we have met, briefly, when we were in South Africa. Just a passing acquaintance. I wasn't well at the time and not feeling sociable. That may have led him to have quite the wrong impression of me. So please don't worry on that score, Mrs Carpenter. Whatever Mr Hammond supposes, I'm not so stupid as to turn down what promises to be an excellent commission."

Leon regarded her with an ironic expression. She ignored him.

"Well, if you're sure," Helen Carpenter said, doubtfully. Then, brightening, "And please, I'm Helen. We're not at all formal here. You're a very welcome guest, and while you're at Old Radbourne, we do all hope you'll feel thoroughly at home. I loved your book, by the way. Wonderful pictures. Will you sign my copy for me?"

"Goodness, that's the first time anyone's asked," she said, not knowing whether to be embarrassed or pleased.

She was rescued by a slight, wiry man breezing into the room, his hair speckled with melting snowflakes.

"What a day!" he said, limping rapidly across the carpet and introducing himself as Paul Carpenter, Helen's husband. "Glad you've made it before dark. Brr, I'm frozen. It's a real blizzard out there now. But the animals are all fed and tucked in for the night, though I reckon we might have to dig our way out to them in the morning."

"I'll make tea," Helen said. She frowned at Leon, evidently not entirely convinced by his innocent air, and perhaps sensing undercurrents she was not a party to. "For heaven's sake let our guest get to the fire. And do try to make yourself useful for once. Start making the toast. Paul, love, come and give me a hand would you?"

"Your word, dear cousin, is my command. As always," Leon said meekly to Helen's departing back.

"And pigs might fly," she called over her shoulder.

Unabashed, Leon ushered Polly to a chair. He crouched down, picked up a brass toasting fork and wedged on its prongs a piece of thickly cut bread from a heaped plate sitting on the deep stone hearth. Then, holding the bread to a corner where the logs had burned to red embers, he turned to look at her and said, his voice quiet and serious, "Look, let me say before the others get back, I'd rather have contacted you myself, but I was right, wasn't I? Whatever you told Helen, I know you'd have turned down the chance of coming here if I'd made the offer."

"Does it matter? I'm here now."

"And stuck with us. Maybe for more than one night. That's something I didn't plan for, I'm afraid. If there's snow about we're always the first to be cut off. The lane from here to the village soon gets blocked and the gritting lorries always leave us till last."

"Now you tell me."

"But I am glad you're here, Polly. I really do want you to take pictures of my house."

He removed one piece of toast and stuck another piece of bread on the prongs. Firelight glowed on his face, throwing the features into harsh relief. Old Nick himself, crouching over glowing logs complete with toasting fork, she thought sourly. Horns and a forked tail would complete the picture nicely.

The heat from the fire was getting to her. After the strain of the journey, the comfortable chair and the tantalising aroma of toasting bread seemed to be taking the edge off her indignation. The grey-muzzled labrador plodded over and flopped down on to her feet with a companionable lick of her ankle. She reached down and fondled his soft ears.

"You'll like the house, I promise." Her head jerked up. He was leaning towards her . . . far too close. She felt the shivery tension that made her want to shrink back in her chair, but she held herself steady, holding his gaze. "It's a little gem," he said. "Seventeenth-century and pretty well unspoiled. It's built on the site of an earlier manor. There's a medieval barn and dovecote at the back and some fine plasterwork ceilings. It's a house that's always been loved, Polly." Despite his nearness, she felt herself distracted by his obvious sincerity. He might have connived to get her here but he evidently cared very much for his house and his intensity undermined her resentment. "I don't want some unfeeling hack running riot around the place. Old Radbourne deserves – needs – sensitive and intelligent treatment. And I know that's exactly what you'll give it."

She wasn't going to let him off the hook that easily.

"I'll do what I came here to do," she said coolly. "But I'll tell you this for nothing. I don't take kindly to being tricked."

"I think the end will justify the means in this case." His smile held a hint of smugness. "I want the best for Old Radbourne. You can give me the best. Speaking professionally, you must feel just a little flattered."

"Speaking professionally," she answered calmly, "your toast's on fire."

"Oh, hell!"

While he fanned out the flames she glanced at the window. The murk was deepening, dusk closing in early. Huge flakes flung themselves at the glass, slithering down to join the thick white ridges that outlined every small pane. She looked back at Leon Hammond. Each tingling nerve end warned her to keep her distance, yet what could she do? She was stuck here and, dammit, she wanted this commission. The atmosphere of the house already exerted a warm fascination. She wanted to know more, to be given a chance to explore. Already she'd noted the splendid octagonal window in this room, wondering if it was repeated on the upper floor. And the stone carving set into a panel over the hearth, surely that pre-dated the seventeenth-century? Another trace of the earlier, medieval house?

"We really ought to unload your car once we've sampled Leon's burnt offerings." Paul said, returning with a laden tray and closely followed by Helen. "Then we'd better get the car into shelter. I'm afraid if we leave it where it is, we won't be able to find it in the morning."

Polly was appalled when they eventually went out to get her gear. It was far worse than it had been when she'd arrived, a blinding, whirling whiteness that made even the short dash from the front door a hazardous undertaking. The two men helped her to get everything in, and she was more than grateful to hand the keys to Paul so that he could garage the car round the back of the house.

The house seemed extra welcoming after the icy wildness of the blizzard outside and the room Helen showed her to was a delight. There was a faded wallpaper of graceful birds and leaves on the walls. "Georgian, in the Chinese style," Helen told her. "It was discovered in remarkable condition under some Edwardian panelling that was full of woodworm. Leon's had experts in to restore it." The colours, soft pinks and blues, had been picked out in an old French carpet, with the same toning fabrics at the window and on the coverlet and hangings of a splendid half-tester bed. The adjoining dressing room had been skilfully converted into a luxurious bathroom. Polly, who had seen and photographed much glossy but ham-fisted conversion work, recognised a sure and loving hand. No strident tarting up, but a modest blending of the gracious old and the quietly luxurious new.

When she returned downstairs, Leon was in the hall lighting a fistful of candles in a silver candelabra. Helen rolled her eyes in passing.

"Brace yourself, Polly," she called. "You're going to get the party piece. The full *son et lumière* treatment."

Somewhat mystified, Polly watched him switch off the main lights so that the only illumination was the sudden soft flare of candlelight. He picked up the candelabra, holding it dramatically aloft.

"The best way to capture the atmosphere of Old Radbourne is to dismiss the twentieth century."

He was absolutely right. Polly felt her excitement quicken as he swept her from room to room, bringing to life with anecdotes and thumbnail sketches, the lives of the people who had loved and married and laughed and dreamed here down three long centuries. She had to hand it to him, he was a natural showman – probably why he'd done so well on television. And candlelight *was* the perfect medium, throwing deep flickering shadows, warmly illuminating a picture, a piece of furniture, an example of plasterwork. This atmosphere, this particular light, was something she must capture.

"Look," she said, "would you mind if I got my camera? I'd like to try some shots of the drawing room and dining room. Purely experimental, but worth a try. Could you get some more candles?"

She forgot about him as she set up the Hasselblad on the tripod, positioned reflectors, squinted through the viewfinder, checked the light meter. She ordered him to move candles, rearrange chairs and ornaments as though it was Kate helping her. She became totally absorbed, as she always did when a project caught her imagination. She didn't even notice that Leon was as absorbed in watching her at work as she was in her photography. And when Helen was noticed lurking by the dining-room door, waiting for her to finish so that she could bring in supper, she was amazed at how time had raced by.

"No problem. It's a fairly moveable feast," Helen assured her.

"Kate, my assistant, says that when I'm concentrating nothing short of earthquake, fire or flood ever disturbs me." Polly admitted. "But I've just about got what I want, I think. I'll pack up now."

"I like to see that kind of dedication," Leon said quietly. "It confirms my opinion that you're right for Old Radbourne, Polly."

His eyes held no mockery, only a quiet seriousness that caused her to turn away, busying herself with the camera, saying lightly, "Something smells good."

"Only a casserole," Helen said cheerfully. "And lots of home-grown veggies and a good old-fashioned apple pie and cream to finish off. Hope that's okay with you."

"Sounds wonderful," she said, realising that despite the earlier rounds of buttery toast and home-made cake, the delicious smells wafting from the kitchen were tempting her taste buds.

Over the meal she learnt that Leon had bought the house eight years previously. "It came on the market just as I was ready for a complete change of lifestyle." He lifted a wry eyebrow. "One club, one casino, gets to be very like another after a while. I was tired of it all and beginning to consider seriously what I really wanted to do in the long term."

The manor had been run down – woodworm, wet rot, decrepit electrics, leaking roof – because the last of the family who'd owned the house since the early nineteenth century had been a bachelor recluse who'd had no money to spend on repairs. Leon had managed to buy much of the original furniture when it went to auction, and had set about a full restoration.

"It was love at first sight," he said simply. "The manor needed me as much as I needed it."

She thought about that as she lay in bed later. The wind moaned round the eaves, snow still flurried softly, like the tapping of ghostly fingers against the windows. But friendly ghosts, she thought sleepily, not Kate's clanking, frightening monsters. Amiable. Yes, it was that sort of house. Whatever presences had left their mark on these old rooms, they were benign.

She could well understand Leon being enamoured of the place. It was a house that she could easily fall for herself . . .

The room was full of reflected light when she awoke. She went to the window and drew back the curtains. The sky was lightening to a hard steely blue. The landscape flowed away down a wooded valley that was smoothly blanketed in white. The blizzard had passed in the night, leaving a magical arctic stillness.

She bathed and dressed and hurried downstairs, homing in on the tantalising smell of frying bacon. She found Helen, cheerful and chatty, standing by the Aga in the kitchen.

"Sleep well? Good. Bacon and eggs suit you? Help yourself to whatever fruit or cereals you want. I shouldn't bother waiting for the men. They might be a while. They're seeing to the menagerie." She scooped bacon rashers and a couple of eggs on to a plate and passed it over. "All good, local stuff," she said. "Leon rents some of his land to the organic farmer next door. So we get the bacon and pork from him, and most of our vegetables. The eggs are from our own free-range, highly pampered hens."

Polly set about her breakfast with gusto. "You have a lot of animals here?"

"Apart from the hens, a couple of pensioned-off ponies are the permanent residents, but the bulk of the work is with the wildlife emergency hospital Leon set up a few years back." She pressed Polly to a warm, crusty home-made roll and sat down at the table with a mug of coffee. "It started, literally by accident, with a hedgehog that had been hit by a car. After that it just sort of happened. Local people started to bring in orphaned and damaged birds and animals, most of which are treated and either sent on to more suitable long-term sanctuaries or released back into the wild. So there's always a shifting population of sick or injured birds and beasties to attend to."

"I must take a look," Polly said.

Helen laughed. "If you don't, you'll be frogmarched down there. Leon considers it compulsory viewing, especially the road casualties, for all our guests. He reckons if it makes even one driver slow down and take more care on country roads, it's a worthwhile exercise."

"And you and your husband help with all this?"

She nodded. "In a way, we found sanctuary here, too." She sipped her coffee and smiled. "I'm a cousin of Leon from the impecunious branch of the family. We lived quite near each other when we were children and we've always got on well. He came to our rescue at a time when . . . well, we'd had a run of bad luck. He wanted reliable help here and we needed somewhere to live after we lost our business."

"Oh, dear," Polly said sympathetically. "It's always risky, isn't it when you set up on your own? I wonder sometimes how I ever dared take the plunge. Fortunately, at present, everything seems to be on a roll. I just hope it lasts."

"And why not when you're so talented?" Helen said stoutly. "I'm afraid our business was far more prosaic. Just a small garage and car-repair business. Neverthless, it provided us with a living. We were settled and happy. But a bad accident put an end to that." She gave a little shudder. "A hit-and-run driver when Paul and I were walking back from the local pub one night. Paul was in hospital for months. I expect you've noticed he has quite a bad limp."

"Yes, I had. How awful. Were you hurt, too?"

"Only had superficial cuts." She hesitated, her eyes darkening with pain. "But I . . . I lost the baby I was carrying." She stared down into her cup. "They found the stolen car abandoned twenty miles away. Never caught the driver. Anyway, to cut a long story short, it was all too much. I couldn't cope with the trauma and the business just went to pot. We were forced to sell it for peanuts. We were completely broke. That was when Leon offered us a new life here." Her tone was light, matter of fact, as though she had come to terms with her grief and was resolutely putting the past behind her. "It was the saving of us both. I think I'd have had a complete breakdown if we hadn't moved here when we did." She smiled. "We've had a marvellous two years at Old Radbourne. And one day, I suppose, we'll have to think about leaving. Not that we could go just yet. Someone has to stay and look after the place when Leon's away, as he so often is."

"But surely if there's work here and you all get on well . . . and the place is big enough for all of you."

"Now, yes. But if Leon remarried, that would be different. More coffee?" She refilled Polly's cup. "There's no saying if the second Mrs Hammond would want us hanging around."

"And will he remarry?"

"Who's to say?" She smiled mischievously and Polly caught a glimpse of family likeness. That wicked glint in Helen's eyes was remarkably similar to the one she'd noticed in Leon's. "There are enough wannabes. Not that any of them stays around for long. So far, that is. But I'll say this . . . If he goes for a Celia clone, then I'm off, regardless. She was absolutely gorgeous-looking, of course, but she'd a poisonous tongue and what few brain cells she possessed were dedicated purely to satisfying her personal lust for spending money on herself. And could she spend. Phew! Leon was well rid of her. Not that he could see it at the time. But then he was very young and she was pretty dazzling. But I think, by the time she left, he was beginning to question the lifestyle she demanded. Though his pride was certainly hurt by her defection."

Polly remembered Aunt Hester's gossip. "Didn't she run off with a Greek tycoon, or something?" she said, helping herself to another roll.

"Yep. Millionaire ship owner. I think that was a couple of husbands back." Again that wicked spark in her eyes. "The last I heard she was divorcing number three in favour of a Texan oil baron. Still, her abrupt departure from Leon's life did one good thing: it gave him the kick in the pants he needed to start rethinking his life." She put down her coffee mug and stared around the kitchen with its bunches of dried herbs and flowers hanging from the dark beams, a huge antique oak dresser displaying blue and white china along one wall, the range of practical oak cupboards and units along the other, old and new blending comfortably together. "Joking apart, though. I can't say I relish the prospect of leaving all this. I do love it here. The house has such a lovely atmosphere."

"It certainly has," Polly said. Even on short acquaintance it was possible to feel the pull of the place. It made her more determined than ever to do Old Radbourne justice. Not only because Leon Hammond expected the best from her, but because her own imagination had been fired by the house and its idyllic setting. And she'd been handed a gift with the snowfall. She must make the most of it.

As soon as she'd finished breakfast, she wrapped up and took the Hasselblad outdoors. It was bitterly cold, the wind from the north-east like a knife, but she tramped up the hill opposite the front of the house, slithering and sliding, with the snow almost topping her wellies in places. It was worth it though. She felt exhilarated by being outside, alone, in the white and glittering landscape. And she was right. There were some fantastic shots to be had from up here – the house nestling deep among snow-burdened trees and shrubberies, the dark plume of smoke from the sitting room chimney dark against the hard blue sky. The light was terrific.

The cold was biting into her hands by the time she'd run off a roll of film. She knew there was a chance of camera shake without the tripod, but she hadn't wanted to load herself up too much in these slippery conditions. But it was worth a try. She retraced her footsteps down the hill, then set off on a tour of the grounds. She was carefully focussing on a crumbling carved stone balustrade that cast curious shadows over the untouched snow and thinking that she really ought to go in and fetch the tripod, when she caught a glimpse of a tall bulky figure out of the corner of her eye. He had one gumbooted foot on the bottom step of a flight that led to a lower level of the garden, one shoulder propped against a stone urn.

She wondered how long Leon had been standing there, watching her, and promptly ruined the shot. She wound the film on and tried again. Better this time but not perfect. She gave up. Her arms were getting tired. She did need the tripod.

She frowned at him. He straightened up, beckoning. "Come and look at the animals," he called.

Well, why not? Wouldn't hurt to take a breather.

The low sun was in her eyes as she scrunched her way across the terrace to the top of the steps. She started cautiously down the steps, but her foot slithered on the second tread and threw her off balance. His hand shot out and caught her arm. Through the thickness of her padded anorak and the sweater underneath, she felt the hard bite of his fingers. She regained her footing, then stood for a moment rigid in his grasp, feeling herself tense from the sudden jolt and from the unexpected contact.

"Careful," he said, releasing her. "Don't want you breaking your neck."

"Never mind my neck," she said lightly, wishing he'd not stand so close looking as though he was ready to catch her if she slipped again. "My insurance company wouldn't have appreciated a modified Hasselblad."

"Better keep an eye on Hazel, then."

"Hazel?"

"One of the goats in temporary residence. She'll eat anything. Probably enjoy a nice expensive camera by way of a mid-morning snack."

She laughed at the thought. "Over my dead body," she said, negotiating the last step without incident.

"You should do that more often," he said.

"What?"

"Laugh," he said. "It suits you. No, no. There you go, frowning again. Your forehead will look like corrugated cardboard by the time you're forty." He leaned towards her, so close his breath fanned her cheek and murmured in a seductive voice, "Laughter lines, on the other hand, are so sexy and attractive in a woman. Honest. Think about it."

Before she could think of any sort of put-down, he was off, taking long, loping strides across the snow covered lawn.

The . . . the bumptious toad! Who did he think he

was? God's gift to women? Not looking like he did this morning, that was for sure. He'd obviously not bothered to shave and he had on an ancient duffel coat disgustingly splattered with dried mud – or worse – and a nasty, black, moth-eaten woolly hat pulled down to his eyebrows. He looked like a tramp. And he had the cheek to make remarks about her!

"Come on," he yelled. "Hazel's waiting. And there's a barn owl I want you to meet."

She nearly turned and went the other way. But curiosity – and a reluctance to let him see that he'd needled her – forced her to stamp after him. Muttering under her breath she followed to the big barn behind the house, where he'd opened the top half of the door. Coming up to him, Polly looked inside and saw three peacefully browsing lop-eared goats penned in one corner, and a small flock of hens scratching about the floor or flapping on to the bales of hay and straw stored in another part of the barn.

"The hens are resident," he said. "The goats' owner – an old lady in the village – died last week. We're just housing them until they go to a proper goat farm." He pointed. "Our other resident's up there. Can you see him?"

She peered up to where he pointed. At first the bird was hard to spot in the shadows. Then she spied him, roosting high up in the far corner on a beam.

"Oh, yes," she breathed.

"He's a young barn owl. With the aid of local farmers and landowners, we're trying to establish a few breeding pairs. This one's settled in very well. He has access to the big wide world through a hole under the roof and hopefully he'll find a mate in the spring." He closed the door quietly. "Now for the hospital proper."

Another barn, longer, divided into pens and cages,

most of them occupied with an assortment of damaged wild creatures. They walked slowly down the wide corridor between the cages, and immediately all thoughts of herself, and her irritation with him fled. She was far too absorbed in what he had to tell about her about the history of each bird or animal, and its prognosis.

"Your vet's bills must be quite something," she said, when they got to to the last cage where a kestrel with a splinted wing glared fiercely at them from its perch.

"Not to mention the diets of some of these beasties," he said. "Still, what's the use of having money if you don't spend it on worthwhile projects?"

"In the plural?"

"I do have a few other committments."

"Such as?"

"Such as creating a wood on part of my land. Planting with indigenous species is already well in hand. I shall leave most of it to grow in as natural a state as possible but a couple of acres I shall start coppicing when the trees have got to a suitable size. That way the trees live to grow again to provide wildlife shelter. This summer we'll be starting on damming a small stream to provide a series of ponds and marshy areas to encourage amphibians and wildfowl. As for the wild-flower lawns in the gardens, they're already paying dividends." His voice was warm with enthusiasm. "We sowed big areas – oh, three years ago – now in spring and early summer they're terrific. Full of colour and scent. As beautiful in my eyes as any herbaceous border. And, with all the gardening here totally organic, insect, animal and bird friendly to boot."

"From hedonist to ecologist," she said, as they retraced their steps to the door of the barn. "Some change. Why exactly?"

"There is an element of guilt in there somewhere."
He glanced at her. "My great-great-great-grandfather
made his fortune scarring the Lancashire countryside
with slag heaps from his coal mines. Various other
ancesters expanded the commercial empire by building
mills and factories on any green bits going, and spent
their leisure time blasting birds out of the sky or departing
on safari to slaughter big game in other countries. This"
– his gesture encompassed the pens, the snow-covered
grounds and fields – "and my other work for wildlife
is the only way I can think of to redress the balance in
some small way."

"I think that's . . ."

"Foolish and idealistic?"

She shook her head. "No," she said honestly. "Not
foolish. Not foolish at all."

When Polly got back to her room, her mobile was ringing.
It was Kate. She'd rung last night to make sure Polly had
reached her destination and to tell her that she'd contacted
Mrs Sheppard and had a good long chat. The housekeeper
had said that Charles was certainly no worse and even a
bit brighter in himself. Kate had giggled. "I get the feeling
that the atmosphere is a bit chilly between her and Sister
Irondrawers. I don't think she goes a bomb on having her
nose put out."

"I'm not surprised," Polly had said. "Anyway, thanks
for that. Saves me ringing again tonight. I don't suppose for a minute I'd be allowed to speak to Charles,
and I resent being patronised by Florence Jackboots
Nightingale."

Now Kate informed Polly that she'd made it – if slowly
– to the office this morning. "Pavements are still a bit

dicey, but the roads are clear," she said. "I hear it's still bad down your way, though. You stay put until it's safe to travel, Poll. I can cope."

Polly's phone call to Charles was less comforting.

Mrs Sheppard answered the phone. To Polly's relief it was Charles and not his watchdog who picked up the bedroom extension.

"I'm improving, slowly," he croaked. "My temperature's down a bit today. Thanks for the fruit. I'll get round to it eventually. How's Dorset?"

"Deep in snow. I shan't make it back before tomorrow."

"You shouldn't have gone at all." He sounded disgruntled. "Very foolish, to go chasing down there with that forecast. I'm surprised you didn't think about me . . . how worried I'd be."

"But I'm fine," she protested. "I got here before the blizzard really set in. I've been made very welcome," she said, in an effort to introduce a more cheerful note. "It's a lovely hou—"

"I'm afraid I was too ill yesterday to realise how bad the weather was," he said "or I'd have tried to dissuade you from travelling. And I've been waiting for you to ring this morning."

"Oh, Charles, I'm sorry," she said, guiltily. "I dashed out first thing. Wanted to take advantage of the light and the snow. I've just come indoors."

"Well, no matter." He paused, then said in a more reasonable tone, "I daresay you think I'm getting everything out of proportion. Perhaps I am." He managed a small harrumph of a laugh, which turned to a cough. "But you know how it is. When you're ill and lying in bed with nothing much to occupy your mind . . ."

"I know," she said gently. "But there's no need to worry about me. Just you concentrate on getting better."

"And you'll be back tomorrow?"

"Well, yes. Hopefully."

Polly caught the murmur of another voice in the background, then Charles said, meekly, "I'd better go now. I mustn't get overtired or I'll set myself back. Just so long as you're all right."

Under orders, Polly thought glumly as she put the phone down. Poor Charles, left to the mercy of the dragon. Perhaps she *should* have stayed in London. Made herself available to hold his hand and feed him grapes, and battle Megan Lacey for the privilege.

But there was nothing she could do about it now, was there? She'd made the decision and if, with hindsight, it appeared to be the wrong one then she could blame no one but herself for being so . . . so self-centred. Damn. Why hadn't she considered Charles more and herself less? She brooded guiltily for a bit, mulling over her conversation with Charles, until her eye fell on her travel bag and the packet of prints from the African trip poking out of the top.

Idly she opened the packet and riffled through the prints. Not bad. Not bad at all. She'd go through them properly later. In the meantime, feeling somewhat cheered, she remembered that the day was still young and she had work to do instead of sitting here worrying about Charles and her own lack of consideration.

She took the prints down with her when she joined the others in the sitting room late that afternoon. Workwise, it had been a very satisfactory, if tiring, day. Apart from a quick snack lunch, she'd been outdoors on her own for most of it. But it had been heavy going moving tripod and camera from place to place until the light got too difficult, by which time her feet felt like two ice floes pinioned to the end of her legs. So she had gone indoors to have a hot shower and change before coming down to the welcome sight of the snapping log fire and cosy lamplight.

Helen, curled up in a chair reading a paperback and eating an apple, smiled as Polly stood diffidently at the door.

"Do come on in. I was beginning to wonder if you planned to put up arc lights and carry on taking photographs after dark."

"Now there's a thought," Polly said.

"We could always fix it," Leon said. His feet were surrounded by a litter of books. "Doing a bit of background research for a proposed documentary," he explained, jotting something in the notebook balanced on one black-jean clad knee before he looked up. "Mind you don't trip. I'm not the tidiest of workers when I get going."

"You've got a perfectly good study and heaven knows how much electronic gadgetry, all in the name of research and efficiency," said Helen, with mock crossness, pretending to aim the apple core at him before she relented and tossed it onto the fire. "Yet you spend half your time sprawled about in here with pen and paper and books."

"Can't beat it," he said amiably. "Much more satisfying than pressing buttons and staring at a VDU until you're cross-eyed."

"You're a closet reactionary," said Helen.

"True. I sometimes wonder if I'm a throwback to the age of quill pens and inkhorns." He raised his eyebrows and looked at Polly. "Arc lights?"

She considered for a moment. "Not a bad idea."

"Spring or summer, perhaps, eh?"

"I'll think about it." Would she come back? She wanted to. For the sake of the house, not him. "I brought down my African pictures to show you," she said. "They're only roughs."

She passed round the photographs. Helen oohed and aahed over them. Leon said nothing at all until he'd looked through the lot, then selected five, cleared a space on the small table next to his chair and spread them out.

"I like these," he said. He had an unerring eye. He had picked the cream of the bunch. He tapped a finger on the table. "That one in particular."

"Oh, no," Helen protested. "Too morbid. The one with the lion cubs is much nicer."

"Chocolate-box stuff," he said, shaking his head. "This has a different quality altogether."

She had taken it near one of the game lodges. A troop of baboons was crossing a track, one female carrying a newborn baby. But the baby was dead, its limbs hanging flaccid, head lolling. Somehow the camera had captured the poignancy of the mother clinging tenaciously to her dead infant while other young baboons leapt about her, uncaring, and vibrant with life.

If Polly had had to choose one photograph that represented her whole African safari experience it would have been that. The stark reality of life and death, the natural unrelenting rhythm of nature encapsulated in one photograph.

"Come on," Leon said suddenly, shuffling the prints back into the envelope. "I have something I want to talk over with you."

She followed him into his study. She had glimpsed it briefly on his *son et lumiere* tour, booklined and untidy with heaps of papers and files spilling off chairs, and an up-to-the-minute workstation wedged into one corner.

"Doesn't exactly go with the seventeeth-century atmosphere," he said, jerking a thumb at it, "but, unfortunately, twenty-first-century communications are a necessity. And it does have its uses, not least when it comes to collating my notes. Like this lot, for example."

He handed her a wad of papers before scooping an armful of books off a scuffed leather chair so that she could sit down.

"What is it?"

"I've been working on it for the last year in my spare time. The story of the restoration of the manor, how the animal hospital started, my plans for the woodland . . . All the stuff we've talked about while you've been here." He pulled open a drawer and produced a stack of photographs. "These are snaps I've taken myself. Not in your class, of course."

"Not bad," she said, leafing through them slowly.

"One or two will pass muster. But, more to the point, will you read what I've done so far of the manuscript and tell me if you'd be prepared to work with me?"

"How?"

"For one thing photographing the animals. Before and after shots, that sort of thing. The vet treating them. I warn you, though, some of it can be distressing."

"But it isn't really my scene."

"You can't possibly say that. Not with the pictures you've just been showing me."

"We're talking collaboration here." She eyed him sardonically. "What were you telling me about choosing my next collaborator?"

He grimaced. "Hoist with my own petard. Well, if you

113

think it's a load of rubbish, tell me straight. I'll try to bear it."

"Practically speaking, I think I should have to refuse anyway. Think of the time I'd lose travelling up and down here regularly."

"You could come here weekends. Stay a couple of nights. Back to London Monday morning. Make it whenever you could fit it in round your other work."

"But the cost . . ."

"Hang the cost! This is something I desperately want to do. And I've got a publisher interested." He was pacing up and down in front of her as he talked, intense, eager, radiating an enthusiasm that was undeniably contagious.

Careful, careful, an inner voice cautioned. *Don't get carried away. The less you have to do with him the better.*

"Look, will you at least read the manuscript?" He stopped in front of her, a slow smile spreading over his bony face. "One thing I'll promise you, it'll be a damned sight more readable than your Charles's thesis on follies."

"There's modesty for you."

"I'm a realist," he said. "I know what I'm good at. I'm also well aware of my failings, which are many. And you have to admit that I was spot on about the follies book. You got the praise, Gregson got the stick. Right?"

She bristled. "Not totally. One critic said it was very worthy."

"Worthy?" He threw back his head and laughed. "Big deal. I ask you, who's going to read a book on that sort of recommendation? A few scholarly recluses? Now my book—"

"Don't tell me. I'll supply the adjectives. Brilliant! Fantastic! Superb!"

He bent over her. "My book will be written for one purpose: to drive home my ideas on ecology and conservation. To make people aware that they have it in their own hands to destroy what's left of our rapidly shrinking countryside, or to treat it with care and consideration. But believe me, it won't read like an educational tract. It'll be light, funny – even a bit racy. Which doesn't mean that the underlying message won't get through. The trick is not to let the reader know he's being brainwashed."

She nodded, said sharply. "That sounds about right for you. Like the business of getting me down here. Machiavellian. Underhand."

He looked startled. Then there was a scratching at the door and Sam the labrador plodded in. He'd taken a shine to Polly and had been following her round while she worked. Now he came up to her and laid his head on her knee, staring adoringly into her face.

She was glad to turn her attention to the dog. She wished she hadn't spoken out. She'd seen the work he was doing here. Approved of it. If she was really honest, she liked the sound of what he proposed to do with the book. But she didn't want to get involved with Leon Hammond more than she had to. Better to make that clear.

"You've made a conquest," he said quietly.

"He's a dear old thing," Polly said, scratching Sam's ears.

"No sense where women are concerned though," Leon said. "He's never learned that they're fickle creatures. Give them your heart and they're bound to break it."

Polly glanced at him. Was he fooling or did she detect an undertone of bitterness? But his mouth was turned down in a mock-dramatic way and there was that wicked glint in his eye that she mistrusted.

"Poor Sam was my wife's dog originally, you see. He gave her the best months of his puppyhood. And what did she do? Run off and leave him lovelorn." Something hard flickered momentarily in the deep-blue eyes. "Enough to put him off women for life. Yet the poor sap still goes on hoping he'll find true love again some day."

She wondered if he was talking about himself or the dog. Underneath the banter there was a trace of bleakness. Celia's defection must really have hurt. She felt an unwanted stirring of sympathy. What had he said? *'The manor needed me as much as I needed it.'* That must have been a horrible time for him. Perhaps he'd flung himself into restoring the manor as a way of forgetting . . .

She pulled herself up short. If he was playing for sympathy she'd be a sucker to fall into that trap. She gave Sam a last, brisk pat and got to her feet. "I'll glance through the manuscript later and let you know what I think about it. But I can tell you this, It'll have to be pretty special to make me take you on as a collaborator. So don't get your hopes up."

"I won't," he said.

"My decision will be based solely on the merits of the manuscript and nothing to do with your emotive and melodramatic machinations, however justified the cause."

"Yes, ma'am," he said meekly.

She wasn't sure whether it was a suppressed sigh or a chuckle as she walked to the door. But she straightened her shoulders and went out without looking back.

*   *   *

The rough, half-completed manuscript was, to her dismay, all that he had promised.

Once she'd settled in bed that night, she picked it up with reluctance, intending to skip through a few pages in order to justify her decision to turn him down. But she found herself hooked. When she switched her light off in the small hours she felt cheated because it ended in the middle of a paragraph. She wanted to get up, bang on his bedroom door and order him to wake up and get the book finished. It was a winner. Absolutely. It had everything: wit, pathos, tragedy, farce, all put over in an easy, fluent style.

She stared out into the darkness long after she'd switched off the light. She wanted to take the photographs. No question. But should she?

Photographing the house was one thing, collaborating with Leon over a book, quite another. One more session, say, in spring or early summer to catch the flavour of the house in a different season, would probably be enough to fulfill her obligations here. And she could be as wily as Leon was. She could arrange it with Helen to be here when she knew he was away. But putting together a book meant there had to be some personal contact.

The less she had to do with him the better. She didn't trust him. But the challenge of working with the birds and animals on a project of this quality was a temptation hard to resist.

She was still prevaricating the next morning. Still unable to resolve the inner struggle. Common sense told her it was to her own advantage to go for it. A deeper, darker instinct warned her to be wary.

"I can't give you my decision yet," she told him, hedging her bets. "I'll have to check my diary before

I commit myself." Then, knowing it had to be said, and trying not to make it sound as though each word was being dragged between gritted teeth, she muttered, "The manuscript was excellent, by the way."

He beamed. "Not too melodramatic? Too emotive?"

"Both," she said.

"But you didn't mind that?"

"In the book, no. In this case I believe the end justifies the means."

"But if emotions escape into real life?" He paused, looking at her from under his black eyebrows, and said softly, "Too uncomfortable, eh? They might worm their way into that glass case where your heart is stored."

"You see, you're off again. Talking melodramatic rubbish."

They were standing at the window at the west end of the gallery above the hall watching a gritting lorry crawl down the road past the manor gates. A soft, thawing wind from the south was blowing this morning. Her escape route was clear. She could leave any time she wanted. The thought made her strong. She didn't flinch as he leant closer to her, even though the black sweater and jeans he wore seemed to soak up the meagre amount of dismal light that penetrated the window from the overcast morning. The gallery was deep in shadow and he seemed a figure from those very shadows.

"One day," he breathed into her ear, "that glass case will shatter. Then you'll have to come out into the world where real people live and love."

"You must have been a *Snow White* fan in your formative years."

"Ah, yes. She of the poisoned apple and the wicked stepmother. And, of course, the handsome prince who broke the spell with a kiss in true fairy tale fashion." He leant closer. His mouth brushed gently against her cheek. "Well?" he said softly, his breath warm on her skin.

She held herself still. "Well what?"

His mouth moved to the angle of her jaw, to her neck, dropping light, barely discernible kisses.

She stared stiffly ahead, forcing herself not to move, nails biting into her palms.

"Don't you feel just the tiniest bit less sleepy?" he murmured. "Doesn't the blood begin to circulate a little faster in your veins?"

"No it doesn't." She put her hands flat against his chest and pushed him away. "And may I remind you of this?" She clenched her left hand and thrust it under his nose. "I'm engaged to be married."

"Ah, the diamond ring," he said, putting his head on one side and surveying her critically. "You know, I wouldn't give you diamonds. Too icy. You should have something to match the fascinating little sparks in your eyes. One perfect, golden topaz perhaps."

"I shall leave as soon as I've packed up my gear," she said brusquely. "I'll send the proofs from this batch in the coming week, then we can discuss the options for a further shoot."

"Or maybe turquoises – the colour of that rather fetching shirt you're wearing. The colour suits you. Pity you have to spoil it with that cardigan. Mind, I have noticed a definite improvement since we last met." He nodded approvingly. "That cream thing you wore last night, now . . ."

She threw up her hands in despair and stalked away from him.

"You're impossible!" she yelled across the gallery.

"Why on earth you think I should want to collaborate with you on a book beats me. You're rude, you're pushy. You're . . . you're . . ."

"Charming? Witty? Fun to be with?" he shouted back.

"Get lost!"

"Sexy? Irresistible?"

"Believe that and you'd believe anything!" She fled to the sanctuary of her bedroom. Because, despite her resolve not to give him an inch and to stay in control, she was about to succumb to a sudden and hysterical urge to giggle.

And that was the last thing she wanted Leon Hammond to see.

Five

The slush washed away in a dirty grey tide into London's gutters leaving the coloured lights, the gold and silver angels, the glitter-laden shop windows to lure the hordes of Christmas shoppers into orgies of spending.

Aunt Hester breezed into town and had an ecstatic few days rifling the Knightsbridge stores.

"Is there anything at all left in the West End?" Polly asked, surveying the mountain of gift-wrapped parcels dominating her aunt's hotel bedroom.

Hester waved an airy hand. "Such pretty things in the shops this year. I couldn't resist."

"I don't believe you tried," Polly said.

"Not too hard," her aunt said complacently, flicking a stray red curl into place. "Shall we go down to dinner?"

"Charles was so sorry not to make it this evening," Polly said as they settled into their seats in the plushy, pink-lit restaurant. "He's still pretty groggy."

Hester ran a scarlet-tipped finger down the menu.

"That's why you're a bit down, is it?" she said absently. "I think I'll go for the grilled sole. Something simple. Then I can justify a hefty cholesterol intake on the puds. Gorgeous creamy things they do here." She fixed Polly

121

with her sharp eye. "Or are you sickening for a cold or something yourself?"

"Me?" Polly said, surprised. "I'm okay."

"You do seem a bit depressed, darling. Rather too quiet."

"Do I?" Polly shook her head, smiling. "I guess it's just that I am a bit tired. It's been pretty hectic since I got back. So much to catch up on. Lots of midnight oil being squandered. Then there's been the worry over Charles."

It was more than that but she hadn't realised it showed. Since she'd returned from Dorset she'd been overcome by fits of restlessness. Perhaps, she'd reasoned, it was a hangover from the African holiday. All that sun, the colour, the excitement must have spoiled her for her everyday routine. Yet she still enjoyed most of her work as much as ever. There was plenty of challenge to stir her imagination and her ambition. Perhaps too much, at the moment, certainly. That must be part of it. She was under the sort of pressure she'd rarely experienced before. Then there was the business of Charles taking longer than expected to regain his full health.

He was pale and languid – and very much inclined to be tetchy in an invalidish kind of way. He was niggly with Mrs Sheppard and petulant with Polly. Only Megan Lacey seemed able to soothe his ruffled feathers.

Her official duties were over but she had been cosily ensconced with Charles several times when Polly had called.

"Had to see how my patient was faring," she would say, with a Polly-excluding smile. "You did give me quite a worrying few days, you know." Her immaculate blonde head would nod at Charles with a horrid archness that made Polly's skin crawl. Her hands were always busy with what she called 'something useful' – embroidery or a piece of knitting. For charity sales of work, she said. One day it had been something shapeless in wool of such a revolting shade of liver-brown that Polly wondered, sourly, if she'd moved into knitting organs for transplants. "Must get it finished for the sale on Saturday," Megan cried. "These handmade cushion covers sell like hot cakes, particularly just before Christmas. I always decorate them prettily with embroidered flowers and beads and I have people coming back year after year asking for more. Of course, drawn-threadwork is my speciality. But it is time consuming and so little appreciated." She sighed. "I'm afraid such feminine hobbies are sadly underrated in the rush of modern living. All that today's young women seem to think of is rushing about competing with men." A sideways flickering glance took in Polly's old jeans, sturdy boots and the bulky anorak she hadn't bothered to take off because she'd only looked in for five minutes. Megan smoothed the skirt of her pastel blue two-piece. "They have no time at all for cultivating the gentler, caring side of their nature."

Polly opened her mouth to argue, then clamped it shut again. Charles, she reminded herself grimly, was still recuperating. Even though he was up and about, he was still convalescent. She had no wish to start an acrimonious exchange and upset him. Especially as he was nodding sagaciously at Megan and swallowing every sugary sentiment. And, good grief, he even seemed to be gazing with approval at her bloody knitting! Or at least making a good pretence at it. Weird. Perhaps the illness had temporarily unhinged his intellect. Otherwise he'd never have allowed the concept of bead-embroidered, hand-knitted liver-coloured cushions to invade the cool minimalist environs of his home.

But even Megan Lacey's poison darts and Charles's irritability didn't totally explain her restlessness. It was something deeper, perhaps to do with the thick layer of tinselly tat that confronted her on every side, with the clogging seasonal traffic that meant long, frustrating delays when she went out in the car, with the noise and bustle of the tides of Christmas shoppers. She felt apart from it, an outsider. As though the fun and laughter weren't meant for her.

"Perhaps I'm just getting too old for Christmas, Aunt Hes," she sighed as the waiter brought their order.

"Nobody should be too old for Christmas!"

Polly shook her head. "Once you stop believing in Santa Claus, the magic goes and never comes back."

"Cynical nonsense," her aunt said. Then, with studied casualness, she added, "And how was Dorset?"

Polly narrowed her eyes.

"Oh, yes, I wanted a word with you about that."

"Any particular reason?"

"You should know."

"Me?"

"If I didn't know you better I'd be taken in by that look of wide-eyed innocence. But I do and I'm not. Whose idea was it that I should be tricked into going down to visit his house yours or his?"

"Tricked, darling. What an unpleasant word."

"So what happened? He rang you for a chat and asked for my phone number . . ."

"He could have rung directory enquiries."

"But so much more convenient to phone you and get a bit of background information at the same time."

"It's true, we have spoken on the phone. Just the once. But I swear, Polly my love, that your name was hardly mentioned. Except that he did ask in passing if I thought you'd be interested in photographing his house. Naturally, when he told me a little about it, I assured him you'd be thrilled. Oh dear, was it a ghastly ruin? Oh dear, I'm so sorry."

"It's a marvellous old place," Polly said. "As you probably very well know."

"So what's the problem?"

"Old Radbourne's owner."

"Too much of a man for you, is he?" Hester squeezed lemon juice over her Dover sole. "Ah, if I were twenty years younger . . ."

"You're bad enough now," Polly said. "You flirted outrageously with him."

"Twenty years ago, darling girl, I wouldn't have had a mere flirtation in mind. More a wild, passionate affair." She smiled seductively. "*Very* passionate. He's got that look in his eye. Smouldering depths, sensuality . . ."

"Please!"

". . . all handsomely packaged in exactly the right mix of macho muscle, good humour, sharp intelligence and, I would guess, a streak of downright soppy tenderness. What more could any woman ask?"

"That's quite enough, Aunt Hes. I don't want to talk about him any more."

"As I recall, it was you, darling, who introduced him into the conversation," Hester said blithely.

"It was not. You asked me about Dorset. Anyway. I wish you wouldn't go on about him. Yuck."

"But, of course, I forget," Hester said smoothly, "you're an engaged woman. You're set on being Mrs Charles

Gregson. And any girl who's settled for marrying a
stuffed shirt with ice-water in his veins and a heart
that beats with all the passion of a North Atlantic cod,
couldn't possibly be interested in a real flesh-and-blood,
sexually potent hunk of manhood."

Polly dropped her knife with a clatter.

"You may be my aunt," she said through her teeth, "but
blood ties can be broken."

"Now Leon—" her aunt began, unabashed.

"I won't listen to another word."

Hester smiled. There was a sly edge to it. "There, there,
darling," she said. "You mustn't get so het up. Bad for the
digestion. I'm sure Leon would be dreadfully concerned
to learn that even the mention of his name has this most
disturbing effect on you."

"If you say anything . . . I mean . . . I'm not in the
least . . ."

"We'll change the subject entirely," Hester said innocently. "You're beginning to look quite flushed. Are you
sure you haven't picked up Charles's germs? Not that
I suppose he ever gets that close to pass them on, but
perhaps viruses can leap on you from a great distance.
Like Olympic long jumpers."

Polly made to get up and leave. Hester beamed and
patted her hand reassuringly. "Did I tell you about this
divine-sounding cruise to the South Pacific I've booked
for February? Such a miserable month in England, I
always think. And I'll be with friends in Cheltenham
for Christmas . . ."

The conversation moved to safer topics. Hester, thankfully, had done with teasing, though the evening did
nothing for Polly's peace of mind. Game, set and match
to Aunt Hester, she thought gloomily. She should have

known better than to fall into that particular trap and let her aunt – champion at these sorts of games – get under her defences.

That man! She consigned him to the bottom of the sea, to the outermost reaches of space, anywhere but in her mind where, like a resident ghost, his dark image seemed to have established itself. When she was busy she managed to forget him, but the minute she relaxed there he was, ready to pounce out of the woodwork.

She was annoyed, worried, angry, in turn. And scared. That, too. Because this haunting was something she couldn't control. It was irrational, perverse – a threat to her peace of mind.

She flung herself into her work. Luckily, she was run off her feet. There was a last-minute panic by a small advertising agency she occasionally did work for. Bread-and-butter-studio photography. This time it was a new line in tableware, delivered to the office in vast boxes that cluttered up the limited space. That shoot had to be completed and the transparencies delivered to the client before Christmas. In fact everybody wanted to clear up business before the break. Then there were the extras: the interview to be recorded for local radio, a quick dash to Oxford with a portfolio of photographs for the proposed spring exhibition, the inevitable Christmas shopping. And, glad that she was to see him better, Charles's recovery meant that she no longer had all her evenings free.

All the same, it was pleasant to be able to relax and forget work when they resumed their regular outings. He was back to his normal courteous self and she thankfully let him take over their plans for Christmas, readily agreeing with everything he suggested, happy that the tetchy little interlude of his convalescence was past. Into every relationship, she told herself, a little rain must fall. They were lucky that most of the time they were happy with each other.

Three days before Christmas, Charles held a cocktail party at his house for business colleagues, their wives, important clients and a few acquaintances to whom he owed hospitality. Polly had been invited in previous years, occasionally dreaming up an excuse because she found this sort of formal function a bit daunting. She'd been last year, but as a guest who could linger with anyone congenial that she happened to meet up with, and leave whenever she wanted. This year she was engaged to Charles and more was expected of her. She'd have to circulate, make sure she spoke to everybody, and there'd certainly be no nipping off if the conversation got a bit difficult or boring.

Still, she comforted herself as she shook hands, made small talk and kept smiling, it was all beautifully organised: a barman hired for the occasion, Mrs Sheppard moving among the guests with trays of canapés, background music playing at exactly the right level, Charles greeting arrivals and introducing guests to each other. The only fly in the ointment was Megan Lacey.

"I felt I should ask her," Charles had explained when she'd spotted the name on the guest list. "She's rather a lonely person, you know."

Polly prevented herself from saying that she was hardly surprised.

"She's an army officer's widow," Charles went on. "She's lived abroad so much in recent years that she's hardly had time to make friends in England. She's no need to work, actually, her husband made ample provision for her, but she's the sort of person who enjoys helping others."

Polly reminded herself that Christmas was the season of goodwill when she was inevitably cornered. She made a big effort to look attentive and interested as Megan, in tasteful beige tonight with pearls at her ears and throat, explained how she was to spend Christmas helping out at an old people's home.

"I did the same last year," she said. "And it was most rewarding to see how pathetically grateful the old souls were for one's modest contribution." She smiled smugly at the recollection. "Mind, I stood no nonsense. Old people can be quite stubborn and set in their ways, I find, quite to their own detriment. And the staff at the home did tend to be rather slack and easygoing, not stimulating their charges with new ideas and interests. In fact, some of the residents were inclined to sneak off to their rooms. I suspect there was a bit of secret tippling going on, but I wasn't going to have the day spoiled for everyone because of a few sluggards. I soon rounded them up to join in the group activities – community singing, suitable games and so on."

Polly's sympathies winged towards the defenceless old people, as yet unaware of the fate about to descend on their comfortable Christmas.

"Bully for you," she murmured with a sarcasm that was quite lost on Megan.

"I also insisted that the television was turned off," she continued merrily. "There was naturally a little grumbling at missing an episode of one of those dreadful soaps, but in the end everyone saw how much more agreeable it was to join in a sing-song or play 'Pass the Parcel'. I never let the fun flag for one moment." She leant confidentially towards Polly. "If one has any sort of social conscience one must lay one's own interests aside in order to attend to the needs of others."

"Must one?" Polly said faintly.

"Which reminds me – and you won't mind me saying this, dear, will you – but there are at least two sets of guests who are becoming rather static."

Polly followed the direction of Megan's gaze.

Puzzled, she said, "They seem to be enjoying themselves."

"Getting a little cliqueish, don't you think? At this sort of event, the hostess" – her expression signalled Polly's unsuitability for this role – "should encourage people to move on."

"Oh, I'm sure—"

"You must be aware, dear," Megan persisted brightly, "that an occasion such as this is only partly social. Now I happen to know – Charles mentioned it to me – that the man in the grey suit and blue tie is an important prospective client that Charles is particularly anxious to impress."

Polly knew that, too. But the man in question seemed perfectly happy chatting up a rather dishy young blonde.

"The young lady, pretty as she is, is of no consequence at all. He should be talking to that fair-haired man, the one Charles designed that block of luxury flats for. He is most enthusiastic about Charles's work. He could well tip the balance in Charles's favour."

"Yes, but—"

Megan's tinkling little laugh rang out. "I can see that you're quite out of your depth, dear. But as the wife of a colonel, one learns to cope with all manner of social occasions and I'm sure I can set everything to rights."

She set off across the dove-grey carpet and, under Polly's fascinated gaze, neatly and smoothly removed the prospective client from his corner, edged him puposefully towards the man she wished him to meet, placed them a little apart from the others, summoned fresh drinks and discreetly left them.

It was like watching a trained sheepdog at work, and the sheep didn't even seem to realise that they'd been cut from the flock and penned in together. Polly felt like giving her ten out of ten and a round of applause, but she saw that Charles, in a manner of speaking, appeared to be doing just that. Megan had moved to his side and he was smiling warmly at her as she whispered in hs ear. They both looked remarkably self-satisfied, Polly thought, feeling sudenly young and useless.

The party was moving smoothly along its preordained track. There was the muted buzz of civilised conversation, the soft murmur of music, the clink of glasses. Polly seemed to be the only one standing alone, marooned on a private island of silence. It gave her an awkward and uncomfortable feeling, as though she were invisible. As though if she slipped away now nobody – not even Charles – would notice or miss her.

The feeling clung to her long after the party was over, which was quite ridiculous because Charles was pleased with the way everything had gone. Pleased with her.

"Thank you, Polly, for being such a charming hostess," he said, when they were alone again. "Everyone keeps telling me how lucky I am." He kissed her gently. "As if I didn't know it already."

But even the warmth of his words didn't quite make up for the feeling of inadequacy which Megan Lacey had induced, and which stayed with her, uncomfortably, for the rest of the evening.

On Christmas Eve she took Kate out for lunch at the nearby pub, where they exchanged silly presents, giggling over their choices, before they hugged each other and parted in a flurry of good wishes, Kate to the boisterous bosom of her extended family, Polly to her quiet house to get ready for her trip with Charles to Marlow where they were to spend a couple of days with the Scotts.

It was a long-standing arrangement: Charles went there most years. But hospitable as the Scotts were, Polly had been half wishing that this year, now they were engaged, she and Charles might have spent the time here in London. Just being together, the two of them. She could have cooked Christmas dinner for him – she enjoyed cooking when she had the time and someone other than herself to cook for. But Charles had brushed the idea aside with a smile.

"The Scotts expect us, my dear. I wouldn't like to hurt their feelings, or upset their arrangements."

"But I'm sure, this once, they'd understand."

"I thought you always enjoyed our visits to Marlow," he'd said in some surprise.

"I do."

"Well, then, I can't see there's any problem." He'd patted her hand. "Besides, it'll be a nice rest for you. You've been rushing around like a scalded hen recently. Do you good to put your feet up and take it easy."

She didn't press it. She didn't want to cause any friction. But she still felt a wisp of regret for the Christmas that might have been.

The small sitting room was full of the delicious piney scent of the baby Christmas tree she'd bought on impulse. A bit silly really when she was going to be away. Still, she and Charles could enjoy it for the quiet hour they'd spend together before they left for Marlow. She was looking forward to that.

After her bath she sat in front of the fire drying her hair, then decided to wear the cream jersey outfit to go to Marlow. She had to hand it to Kate, she thought as she got dressed, everything she'd been bullied into buying had been very useful and comfortable. Except that green skimpy thing. She hadn't had time even to look at it since she'd stuffed it into the back of the wardrobe. In the New Year she really must do something about it. She couldn't afford expensive mistakes like that. She'd have to see if she could swap it for something more serviceable.

She sang along with carols on the radio as she set out the petits fours she'd spent ages making last night, knowing that they were favourites of Charles. They could nibble them as they opened their presents. Charles had suggested that Christmas Eve might be a more suitable time for that than Christmas morning.

"Gifts are such personal, private things," he'd said. "And we're not children, are we? No need to make a fuss."

Eyeing the large, flat, ornately gift-wrapped box that had arrived this morning by special delivery from a very swanky shop, Polly was eager to know what Charles had bought her.

"Something exotic and slinky and sexy," Kate had breathed, fingering the dramatic gold-striped ribbons criss-crossing the package.

Polly had laughed. "Something entirely sensible, I expect."

"From there?" Kate squeaked. "In that sort of wrapping? No way!"

"Probably a nice warm woolly cardie," Polly said cheerfully. "Like the one he gave me for my birthday."

Kate's face fell. "Oh, yes. Very matronly."

133

"It was cashmere," Polly reminded her. "And probably horribly expensive."

"I suppose." She sighed. "And I was beginning to think your Charles had hidden depths."

Polly, despite her protestations, was more than a little intrigued, too. The cashmere cardigan had been presented in discreet wrappings, but with the intervention of his spell of bronchitis he'd probably had no time to fuss over details and had left it to the shop. Whatever. The luxurious wrapping certainly stood out and she put it at the front of the little pile of parcels under the tree.

Charles arrived promptly at six. After the climb up the stairs, he sank breathlessly into a chair. He looked washed out and she felt an anguished tenderness for him. Although he'd been claiming to be back to his usual self this week, it was clear that he was still feeling the after-effects of his illness.

He refused anything stronger than tea and leaned his head back against the cushions and watched Polly through half-closed eyes. He shook his head at the petits fours.

"Sorry, my dear. I've been forced to nibble all manner of unsuitable goodies at the office get-together this afternoon. And my digestion just can't cope with too much rich food at the moment."

"Don't worry," she said brightly, trying not to feel disappointed. "They'll keep in the fridge until we come back. Or should I take them with us, do you think?"

"Oh, I shouldn't think so. Vera is always beautifully organised. There'll be masses of food, and to spare. And if you could turn down the music."

"Sure." She leapt to her feet and turned the volume down to a whisper.

"Thanks." He smiled palely and sipped his tea. "Ah,

that's good. Peace at last. Someone had a CD player going so loud this afternoon that you could hardly hear yourself think. How nice to have nothing much to do in the next couple of days, except to enjoy the quiet pleasure of being with good friends."

"Lovely," she murmured, glad to see the colour beginning to come back into his face.

"Brace us both up for the New Year," he said. "And, by the way, I've accepted an invitation for us both to a New Year's Eve function."

"Really?"

"Yes. Leon Hammond's asked us over."

She almost choked on her tea.

"He's been trying to get hold of you, apparently, but couldn't. Your phone was busy."

"To Dorset?" she managed.

"No, no. He has a loft conversion in a warehouse somewhere near the river. I thought it politic to accept."

She stared at him, trying to control her shock. She'd instinctively played down her visit to Dorset once Charles had got over his tetchiness about her travelling down in bad weather. Apart from giving brief details and Charles congratulating her on such a useful contact as Leon Hammond, the subject hadn't been raised again. Now she wished she'd made more of her antagonistic feelings towards him.

"Do we have to go?" she said in a careful, non-committal tone.

"It might be amusing," he said, his lips pursed in calculation. "And rewarding. For both of us. All those media people – it's to be quite a big affair, I gather – could be extremely useful to know." He nodded by way of emphasis. "*Extremely* useful."

She knew Charles well enough to realise that his mind was made up and it would be very difficult to budge him. He talked on while Polly guarded her expression and seethed inwardly. Apart from a brief formal acknowledgement of the proofs Kate had dispatched to him, Leon hadn't contacted her. Until now. Until he'd gone behind her back – again – and got at her through Charles. All that talk of her phone being busy was baloney. He'd known what the answer would have been if she'd received the invitation instead of Charles.

"Well, we'd better open our presents, hadn't we?" Charles said, glancing at his watch.

She'd invent a rare disease. Fall and break a leg. Anything to get out of going.

"The presents, Polly," Charles said. "We don't want to be too late getting off to Marlow."

But she'd be *with* Charles, this time. Thank heaven for that. And there'd be a crowd to get lost in.

"Yes . . . yes, of course. You open yours first."

She handed him her present. A set of Bach CDs and a discreet silk tie to add to his collection of similar ties. When he'd smiled his satisfaction and thanked her profusely, she reached for the extravagantly beribboned gold box prominently displayed under the tree. Then she stopped. Charles had produced from his pocket a small package sheathed in plain white paper.

"I bought it in rather a rush," he said. "But it can be exchanged if it isn't quite to your liking."

She didn't know why she felt such a stab of disappointment. It was a very elegant set of silver teaspoons. They were antique and valuable. But she had been expecting . . . what? Her glance slid nervously to the other box as she kissed his cheek and thanked him. She tried to ignore it as they unwrapped the other gifts, his and hers. Finally her fingers tweaked the gold ribbon, lifted the lid, rustled among layers of tissue . . .

The card slid out. The writing leapt up at her and somehow she whisked the card away and into the litter of wrappings.

"A little extra something from Aunt Hester," she said in a light, false voice which Charles, thankfully, didn't seem to notice.

"Typical Hester," he said disparagingly. "Terribly over the top."

The satin slid seductively over her fingers as she drew it out. A housecoat. Heavens, no, nothing so mundane. A negligée of deep cream satin crusted with heavy falls of lace. The sort of garment she associated with women who had nothing better to do but lounge seductively on sofas, paint their nails and receive the attentions of passionate suitors.

"Where's your overnight bag?" Charles was saying, rattling his car keys. "Better be making tracks."

"Coming," she said, her breath catching in her throat.

She let the negligée drop back into the box in a creamy sensuous puddle. Among the wrappings the card was visible to her wide, stunned eyes.

The wording, in Leon's bold spiky hand, was already engraved on her mind.

All it said was, "Dare you!"

Christmas Day slipped past anti-climactically, almost as if events had peaked on Christmas Eve at the moment she'd opened that frivolous and unwelcome gift.

The Scotts were tired after the pre-holiday rush at the hospital where they worked. There was plenty of food and drink and various friends dropped in to exchange seasonal greetings, but Polly had the distinct impression that had she and Charles not been there, Tom and Vera would have been content to put their feet up and snooze a great deal of the time.

She felt full of pent up energy. On Boxing Day morning she did her best to persuade them to move from the stuffy sitting room.

"It's drizzling, Polly," Charles said, frowning at the gloom outside.

"Not that much," she said encouragingly. "Do come for a walk. It'll blow away the cobwebs."

He gave a mock shiver. "I'm just over bronchitis," he reminded her gently. "Getting cold and wet is the last thing I need."

She was suddenly impatient with him, and with the Scotts who exhibited mild surprise that anyone should actually choose to turn out on such a miserable day.

She gave up. Without another word she fetched her mac and stalked out. She walked fast, head down, the damp air cooling her hot cheeks. She made her way to the graceful iron bridge that spanned the Thames and then took the path along the river. Overhead the clouds began to break up and, with the clearing skies and the emergence of a watery sun, other people began to come out too: couples, families, children on shiny new bikes clutching new toys.

She stood on the bank and watched the ducks paddling madly from one group of bread-throwing children to another. She was painfully aware of her own solitude. Each family, each strolling couple seemed so self-contained and content. And it was Christmas. No fun in being alone.

She pulled her thoughts up short, trying to be reasonable. After all, she'd chosen to walk out on the others. And who could blame Tom and Vera and Charles for wanting to relax indoors? They were busy people, deserving of a rest. And, a sneaky little voice said, they were a different generation – older – less energetic perhaps. Another word zoomed into her head. She tried to slap it away, but couldn't. Bored. She'd been bored. No, no, no. How could she have been? The Scotts were so kind and hospitable. And Charles . . .

She pulled her hands from her pockets in a fierce dismissive gesture. She stared unseeingly at the leafless willows dipping long branches into the water on the opposite bank. Under her feet the gravelly path seemed to sway and shake. She began to walk quickly, dodging the strollers, wanting to get back to the house. She felt panicky, at the same time sensing that the swift shifting of balance was nothing to do with outside influences but with some subtle alteration within herself. As though a door had opened briefly, revealing an unknown landscape, a frightening panorama of unknowable vistas that made her feel suddenly uncertain and lost.

It was a relief to be back. To sink into an over-stuffed chair, to listen to the ebb and flow of desultory conversation, to be cosy and secure as the light died in the gloomy, forbidding world outside.

Her cold limbs steadily warmed up, but deep inside she was aware of a chilly, uncertain sensation that no amount of exterior heat seemed to shift. And, despite allowing her wine glass to be steadily topped up, nothing seemed to get to the heart of that inexplicable and persistent feeling of loss and confusion.

*   *   *

The days between Christmas and New Year went all too quickly. Both she and Charles had closed their offices for the whole holiday period, but Charles was busy at his drawing board at home with a shopping mall development and Polly was glad of the time to work without interruption in the darkroom. She particularly enjoyed experimenting with the African photographs. By New Year's Eve, she had a final set of prints that satisfied even her critical eye.

As she laid them out on her office desk, she thought involuntarily of Leon, and how he'd approve of them. Then thoughts she'd kept suppressed bubbled to the surface. She imagined him laughing, that wicked glint in his deep blue eyes, as he selected the most unsuitable present he could find in order to embarrass her. She saw his face, eager and boyish in its enthusiasm, in the flare of the candlelight as he showed her round the house. She felt the touch of his fingers on her arm as he steadied her on the snow-slippery steps, the brush of his lips against her cheek that last morning at Old Radbourne.

She stared at the dismal grey day outside the windows. Tonight she would have to meet him again. Why, oh, why, hadn't Charles pleaded another engagement?

The phone on her desk rang. She picked up the receiver, expecting it to be Charles or Aunt Hes or Kate. Not him. Not Leon. But it was. And there seemed a strange inevitability about it. She felt herself unsurprised. As though her thoughts and his had made some connection beyond the telephone wires.

"All set for tonight are you, Polly, my love?"

"I'm not your—"

"No, no," he agreed gravely. "You belong heart, soul, liver and lights to the estimable Charles."

"I don't *belong* to anyone. I'm not a parcel, a possession." Even as she spoke, she knew she was rising like a trout to the bait.

"I'm glad of that," he said. "It leads me to believe there's hope for you yet."

"Speaking of parcels," she said, "I've a bone to pick with you."

"If it's anything to do with bones, you'll have to speak to Sam. He presents his own bones to the women he's dotty about. How did it arrive? By dog sled?"

The giggle rose unasked into her throat.

"I'm not talking about your dog or his bones," she managed after a moment wrestling for sobriety. "But that Christmas present you sent me."

"Ah, yes. I had the devil's own job to find exactly what I wanted. You liked it?"

"Whether I liked it or not is immaterial. I couldn't possibly accept it."

"Why not?" Leon enquired politely. "Are you frightened that the sight of you wearing it might inflame your fiancé's passions?"

"Please! I'm trying to have a sensible conversation—"

"It isn't the season for being sensible," he said. "If Charles doesn't approve, wear it when you're alone – and think of me."

"I most certainly will not!"

He sighed. "You're a hard, unfeeling creature." He paused then said softly, "You'd look beautiful in it."

"Huh!"

"Does that mean that you don't believe you could look beautiful?"

"You're being ridiculous."

"Beauty is in the heart, Polly as well as in the bones."

His voice was a caressing whisper. "You've convinced yourself you're plain, and dress like a frump just to prove it to the world. But for anyone with eyes to see—"

"I can't see any point in this conversation. I'm hanging up."

"I only wanted to make sure that you hadn't invented a fictitious cold to prevent your coming to my party."

It was so near the truth that she was glad he couldn't see the colour in her fiery cheeks.

"I'll be there," she said clearly. "I couldn't possibly let Charles down."

"Good," he said. "I hope we don't miss each other in the crush. I've rather gone overboard with the invitations." A small silence then, "The walls of the flat, by the way, are a sort of mushroom colour."

She frowned. "So?"

His laughter was soft in her ear. "Well, you might want to wear something that blends with the background so that nobody notices you're there."

She slammed down the phone. Indignation sustained her as she took her bath. She sloshed water about furiously, wishing she could throw a bucketful over Leon's head. Why was he doing this to her? She'd done nothing to encourage him. Nothing! He was rude and brash and impossible. She hated him!

She towelled herself dry and padded to the wardrobe. She rattled the hangers noisily, pulling out her new outfits and throwing them on to the bed.

'You might want to wear something that blends into the background so that nobody notices you're there.'

How dare he say such stupid things! What did it matter to him what she wore? And where had she heard these opinions aired before? She didn't have to think very

142

hard. Aunt Hes. Had they been discussing her? She wouldn't put it past either of them. How . . . how sly and deceitful and . . . treacherous. She didn't care about clothes. Why should she? Her priorities lay elsewhere. How could he – they – invent this rigmarole about her wanting to hide herself.

Into the frenetic whirling of her thoughts came a tiny cold voice which said, very clearly, *But you don't exactly like to be the centre of attention, do you, Polly Burton?*

Dammit! She was being brainwashed.

Her hand fell on the last dress left in the wardrobe. The green dress Kate had talked her into buying from her designer friend.

She stared at what there was of it, which wasn't much. She took a deep breath and in one quick movement yanked it over her head. It slid down and settled like a second skin, leaving her shoulders and a good deal else on view. But the cut of it, the way it clung in exactly the right places gave her figure an undeniable and unexpectedly curvy lissomness. On the hanger it looked nothing much. On her . . .

She gulped. Then, as though possessed of a courage that might leave her if she thought about it too long, she got out the make-up Kate had given her and applied eyeshadow, liner and mascara, blusher and lip gloss.

She brushed her still-damp hair fiercely. She still hadn't got round to cutting it and now, lying loose to her shoulders, it crackled with life, the light catching the rusty glints in its brown depths. There was some jade jewelry somewhere. Aunt Hester had brought it back from one of her Far East trips. It had never been out of the box. She clipped on the earrings, fastened the slim gold chain with the fragile green pendant round her throat.

The woman in the mirror stared back at her wearing a bemused expression. Who was this stranger? This person with the shining eyes, smoothly accentuated cheekbones, glossily curving lips parted in disbelief.

Her gaze dropped. She gasped as her hands flew to cover her cleavage. She couldn't go out like this. There was far too much of her on public display. Charles would have a fit.

The doorbell. She leapt to her feet, dithered wildly for a minute, then grabbed her old trench coat, buttoned it to the neck and tottered in the unfamiliar skyscraper heels to meet Charles.

She switched off lights as she went downstairs, kept her face turned from the street lamps as he kissed her cheek and held the car door open. She slid inside and clasped her hands in an attitude of prayer. An electricity blackout, a tornado, a swarm of killer bees . . . anything to halt their journey right now so that she could go back inside, scrub off the paint and remove the disastrous, revealing dress.

The car purred smoothly through calm traffic. The damp evening remained free of violent insects and freak weather. Her nervousness increased as Charles parked the car in the forecourt of the warehouse conversion and as he took her arm to lead her inside she cast a yearning look at the river, a silent ribbon shimmering with reflected lights, moving placidly on its untroubled course to the sea. Would that she were on it, in a liner bound for the antipodes.

Leon's apartment was on the top floor. It was awash with noise and people. Leon stood just inside the door, greeting his guests. Her stomach lurched when she saw him. She hung back behind Charles, glad that several other people came in at the same time and she could quickly escape to the bedroom set aside as the ladies' cloakroom. She was conscious, all the same, that he hadn't missed her unobtrusive entrance.

She wanted to hide, she wanted to cower in the bedroom with her coat firmly buttoned to the neck, but all around her women were shrugging off jackets and coats to reveal their party clothes. From wisps of dresses far scantier than her own to theatrically dramatic outfits that would have gladdened Kate's unconventional heart, and a whole range of pretty outfits in between. At least she wouldn't be too conspicuous.

She began to breathe more easily as she gingerly peeled off her coat. There were no more than friendly glances cast in her direction. She was only one of the crowd after all.

She spent an inordinately long time rearranging her hair which refused to do anything but spring from her head in a tangle of its own. Then the moment couldn't be put off. She went to find Charles.

He was already deep in conversation with a woman who was introduced to Polly as a television researcher. After a few moments the woman spotted friends and excused herself. Charles turned to Polly with a note of satisfaction in his voice.

"I knew that this evening would turn out to be rewarding. A useful contact there, already. She's involved with a programme on inner city development and was most interested in my views. She's taken my card for future reference." His satisfied smile suddenly disappeared as he focussed properly on Polly. "I . . . er . . . that is . . ." He stopped, cleared his throat, his thin nostrils flaring fastidiously. "I haven't seen that dress before."

"No," she said, feeling herself shrink from his accusing gaze. "It was something Kate persuaded me to buy."

"I might have known." A pained look crossed his finely-drawn features. "It isn't really your style, my dear, is it?"

Something about his expression, his patronising tone, caught her on the raw.

"Why?" she said sharply. "What is my style, Charles?"

"Well, not this sort of thing." He gestured dismissively at the dress. "Far too – er – blatant."

"Blatant? Do you mean sexy?"

She didn't know where the irritation was coming from but it was there, rising like a hot tide, sweeping away the awkwardness, the nervousness she'd felt earlier.

"Now that you mention it, yes. I don't like to see you looking so . . . so tarty." His mouth snapped shut like a trapdoor.

A tray of glasses was thrust between them. Polly took a glass of white and swigged it down in a couple of gulps, choked, and felt even hotter.

"You still haven't explained what you think my style is," she hissed.

"You're a natural, quiet sort of girl," Charles began in a hurt voice.

"Ordinary? Plain? Dull? A nonentity in fact."

"I didn't say that, Polly."

"You meant it."

He stared at her in bewilderment.

"Why are we quarrelling? What's the matter? You're not usually snappy like this."

She shrugged. As suddenly as it had risen, the anger faded.

"I don't know," she said miserably.

"Has something upset you?" He moved closer to her. "Is it this?" His gesture took in the steadily thickening

146

crush, the increasing noise. "Yes, perhaps it is. It's hardly us, is it? Perhaps it was a mistake, like your unfortunate dress. I can't hear myself think and the party's hardly got going. I hate to think what it will be like later. I tell you what, we'll make our excuses and leave. Say you've got a headache or something."

It was what she wanted, wasn't it? She gnawed the inside of her lip, her glance irresistibly drawn to that tall figure, dark head in profile as he talked to a willowy Nordic blonde. Seeming to sense her look he turned, caught her eye and a slow smile spread over his face.

It was impossible he should know what was going on in her mind, but she felt that he knew she was contemplating running away because she was tarted up and scared.

But she wasn't going to run off like a frightened mouse. Nor was she going to blend into the wallpaper. She was going to stay at the party and show him that she was enjoying herself, even if she hated every single minute.

"Sorry I was so ratty Charles," she said meekly. "And you're right, of course. The dress really isn't me. Still, while we're here . . . well, I'm okay now and I'd hate to think of you missing anyone who could be important to you. You go ahead and circulate." She raised her empty glass. "I'm going to find a refill. Then I'll be doing a little public relations work on my own account."

Charles looked relieved. This was the Polly he knew and admired.

"If you're sure."

"Quite sure," she said with a reassuring smile.

When he turned away to assess the crowd she pushed her way to the temporary bar at the end of the long room. She needed the wine, crisp and cold, to blunt the nervousness that tingled along her nerve ends. Particularly

147

when she became aware that she certainly wasn't destined to be a wallflower that evening.

She hardly knew how it began. Perhaps it was something in herself that threw out an invisible reckless challenge. Perhaps it was just that it was difficult to stay aloof in that crush. But she found herself drawn into conversations, laughing, joking, dancing even . . .

At first she drew back when a complete stranger asked her to dance, but the easygoing young man refused to listen to excuses.

"So you don't dance? Who cares?" He grinned, tugging her on to the cleared square of parquet. "Just jog about in time to the music."

Music pounded out from a hidden sound system and she allowed herself to sway with it. She stumbled a bit at first, feeling stiff and awkward, until suddenly her feet seemed to discover the rhythm and she really was keeping up with everyone else on the miniscule dance floor. And what did it matter if she was making a fool of herself? In this crowd, getting noisier by the minute, there was hardly space to be noticed.

The wine bubbled in her head. She danced and danced again. Different partners, different conversations. She only caught glimpses of Charles, who always seemed to be in earnest conversation with someone whenever she passed near him. She hoped he was getting everything he wanted out of the evening. Just as she hoped, fiercely, that Leon was taking notice of her new social sparkle.

She hadn't seen much of him, either. At least he was having the decency to keep out of her hair. More interested, she suspected, in the Nordic blonde, whose face was vaguely familiar. Someone had said that she was a well known actress called Karen Hill. She'd seen him dancing with her once or twice. When they'd passed on the dance floor he'd given Polly a lazy and definitely approving wink. She'd resolutely ignored him.

The room grew stifling as the evening advanced towards midnight. The wine and the heat had made Polly thirsty. She pushed through the crowd in what she hoped was the direction of the kitchen in search of a glass of cold water. She found the right door, pushed it open, breathed a sigh of relief as a waft of cool air met her, and let the door swing to behind her as she started across what seemed like an acre of glossy tiles.

Then she pulled up short. "Oh," she said. "It's you."

He was leaning against one of the counters, arms folded. The window behind him was wide open.

"Taking a breather," he said.

"I came for a glass of water," she said at the same time.

They both stopped. He smiled. There was a small silence.

"Enjoying yourself?" he asked as his gaze, after taking a slow and apparently interesting route from her feet upward, finally met hers.

"Great party," she said stiffly, shivering as the cold air met her bare shoulders.

The party noises were lessening in the other room. Someone called for hush as a radio was switched on.

"Nearly New Year," he said. "New Year. New beginnings. Can I believe that I'm seeing the new Polly Burton? The butterfly emerging from the chrysalis. The sleeping princess from her glass case?"

"I came for a glass of water," she repeated, forcing herself to take a step towards the sink. He was unnervingly close.

"The new Polly Burton will be an even greater pleasure to work with than the old," he said softly.

"I haven't agreed to anything yet."

"The book's waiting. The animals are waiting. I thought perhaps we could start next week."

"I'll think about it."

"Come for the weekend. We'll look for violets."

"In January?"

"If you know where to look."

In the other room the sound of Big Ben chiming the quarters boomed out. They looked at each other. Then the clang of the twelve slow strokes and a blossoming of noise from outside: sirens hooting from boats on the river, the tooting of car horns, bells ringing. A male voice began singing 'Auld Lang Syne' and immediately every voice in the room next door swelled up to join in.

"Happy New Year," Leon said.

"Happy New Year," Polly said.

He reached out, his hands warm on her upper arms. He drew her close, bent his head. He kissed her forehead under the escaping tendrils of hair. He kissed the tip of her nose. Then, lightly at first, his mouth met hers.

"Beautiful Polly," he murmured against her lips, his hands slipping down her back to draw her close. And for a few mesmerised moments she pressed against him, her mouth opening under his, wanting to be held close, wanting . . . what?

His grip tightened, the roar of happy noise from the other room burst in. Her eyes snapped open and a whirl of lurid colour seemed to revolve in her mind. Colour and shadows and terror . . .

"No!" she gasped. "No, please!"

She was fighting him, pulling away, hardly aware that

150

he no longer tried to hold her but had let her slip easily from him, his face expressionless, his eyes watchful and compassionate.

She turned sharply away from him, her hands covering her face, her shoulders heaving as she struggled to catch her breath.

He didn't move for a moment, then turned and began to reach for more chilled wine out of the fridge, all the time chatting lightly as though he'd noticed nothing amiss.

After a few minutes she was able to walk calmly back into the crush and look for Charles as though nothing had happened.

And after all, what had?

He wished he knew what to do next about Polly.

Leon unhurriedly refilled the fridge with fresh bottles of wine, and closed the door. He should get back to the party. He was the host after all. But he didn't want to, which was tough. It was all going with too much of a swing. It'd be hours yet before he could be on his own again.

He told himself he was a fool. Why did he bother? She was prickly and stubborn and dead set against him. Why not let her sail off into the sunset with her precious fiancé and forget all about her?

He looked at his hands. He remembered how he had felt the slenderness of her bones under the smooth flesh. His eyes still held the image of her face, his mind still felt the siren temptation of those slanting gold-flecked eyes.

He wished he could forget.

But he couldn't.

He wished he hadn't organised this party, either. But he had, dammit. He was out of practice. Out of sync with the whole party bit, if he was honest.

Anne Goring

"Whatever are you doing skulking in the kitchen?"
Karen waltzed across the floor, her spiky heels click-
clacking on the tiles. She flung her arms round him, turned
up her face. "Happy New Year, darling," she murmured.
"Well, come on. Don't I deserve a big, big kiss?"

He obliged. It was very pleasant.

The kitchen door opened again. More people. More
kisses, more masculine handshakes and slaps on the back.
The scents of perfume and wine and the screechy, giggly
chatter of well-oiled voices.

"Marvellous party, Leon," someone said. Others agreed
enthusiastically.

Perhaps it was.

But when he'd opened the chilled wine and taken it
into the other room, Polly had already left. For him the
party was over.

Six

January began with a crisis. One of Polly's best clients, the architectural consortium, went bankrupt owing money everywhere, including a substantial sum to her.

She went gloomily through her accounts then slammed the ledgers shut. She'd have to work on the photographs for Leon's book now. She couldn't afford the luxury of turning down his proposition. She asked Kate to phone and make the necessary arrangements.

"And if he asks, I'm out," she added.

Kate shot her a sharp glance. "What is it with you two? You nearly do a war dance when his name is mentioned."

"Clash of personalities," she said shortly.

"His personality can clash with mine any time," Kate breathed. "I mean, what more could any evilly intentioned female want than a man with terrific looks, fame, money . . ."

"He can keep his fame and his money," Polly muttered, running her eye over the week's appointments and adding, without thinking, "and his stupid presents."

"What presents?"

Polly pretended a deep interest in Thursday's entry but Kate was like a bloodhound on the trail when her curiosity was roused. Polly sighed and told her.

Kate shrieked. "Are you trying to tell me he fancies you?"

Polly glared at her. "No, I'm not. He's got a twisted sense of humour, that's all. Like you."

Kate giggled. "And what did Charles think of his beloved being given a ravishing negligée by a television Adonis?"

"I told him it was from Aunt Hester."

"Aha! The plot thickens."

"The plot definitely does not thicken. It was merely to save Charles's feelings. He might not have thought it as funny as you obviously do."

"I'm darned sure he wouldn't. He'd probably nail your boots to the floor to stop you going down to Dorset for another dirty weekend."

Polly threatened her with a paperweight. Kate disappeared, smirking, into the darkroom.

Kate's words came back to torment her later in the day when Charles rang, asking Polly to keep Saturday free. "I've nearly tied up that shopping mall project," he explained, "but I wanted to meet my client on an informal basis. I've asked him to bring his wife round for lunch on Saturday. You can keep her entertained, I'm sure, my dear, while we talk business. I'm sorry it's such short notice."

"Oh, Charles," she exclaimed, "I can't make it on Saturday. I'm going down to Old Radbourne on Friday evening. I won't be back until late Sunday."

"Is it urgent? Could you postpone it, do you think?"

"If it wasn't for this Lawson crash . . . Well, I can't afford to start putting clients off at the moment. I've got to make up for the loss as quickly as possible."

"I see. Understandable, I suppose." A pause, then,

"Never mind. Can't be helped. I'll see if I can make other arrangements."

"The following weekend would be fine."

"Don't worry about it, my dear," he said kindly. "You've enough to think about. I'll sort something out. Give my regards to Leon, would you? At least you shouldn't have such a horrendous journey this time."

Perhaps it was his understanding that made her feel so guilty. Would he have been so supportive had he known who had given her that ridiculous present? Would he have turned all possessive and jealous?

It was hardly Charles's style, she comforted herself. Besides, there was nothing, absolutely nothing, for him to be jealous about. Leon was merely amusing himself at her expense. She, however, found no amusement in his antics.

This weekend she intended to make that clear in no uncertain terms.

After work on Friday she stuffed the gold box containing the negligée into an undistinguished plastic carrier, and threw it into the car along with her weekend bag and the necessary camera gear. She'd be glad to get the damned thing out of the way. She'd left it at the bottom of her wardrobe, but every time she opened the door she never failed to catch a glimpse of it in the corner. If glitter could look furtive, that gold box did. Or perhaps the furtiveness was just a reflection of her own feelings towards its contents because she felt so guilty about deceiving Charles.

Still, it would soon be back where it belonged. With the clown who'd sent it.

She hummed along to Kiri as she battled the rush-hour

155

traffic. Once clear of the London fringes, the drive through the damp, misty dark was uneventful. No possibility that she would be trapped by snow at Old Radbourne this weekend. After that brief, icy spell in December, the weather had turned unseasonably mild and it seemed likely to continue. She felt calm, in charge of herself and the situation, as she drove through the manor gates and saw the lights glowing softly through the mullioned windows.

The air was gentle against her cheeks when she climbed out of the car. She took deep breaths of the sweet, earthy, country scents. If nothing else, it was good to be out of London for a couple of days. And whatever the foibles of its owner, the house retained that aura of welcome, drawing her into its warm embrace, so that as she greeted the Carpenters and Leon she had the odd feeling that she wasn't merely a transient visitor but an old friend returning to a loved and loving environment.

She tried to explain her feelings to Helen as they stacked the dishwasher after supper.

Helen understood. "I've often thought that houses have distinct personalities. Good and bad." She picked up a tureen and deposited it in the lower basket. "There are places I've been to where I've not wanted to stay for an hour, let alone a day. Like meeting someone who's just not on your wavelength and you don't even want to begin to get friendly with them. Other houses – well, you only have to step over the threshold to feel at home."

"Exactly," Polly said, thinking uneasily of the austere minimalism of Charles's house, in which she'd never quite managed to feel totally at ease. "Old Radbourne certainly comes into the friendly category. It has such a comfortable atmosphere."

"Yes, it has," Helen said. "Paul and I have felt at home here from the very first minute. I can't bear to think about having to leave."

"What's all this traitorous talk of leaving?" Leon said, catching the tag end of the conversation as he came in with the final tray of dirty dishes. "You and Paul are part of Old Radbourne." He put down the tray and looked affectionately at Helen. "Especially now. This is a house that needs children."

Helen blushed. "I'm pregnant," she said to Polly. "I only told Leon yesterday and since then he's gone all broody. I think he's nearly as excited as Paul."

"How wonderful," said Polly, remembering the sad events that had led to Helen losing her first baby. "You must be thrilled to bits."

"You bet," Helen said happily.

"I was beginning to think they'd never make me an uncle – well, a second-cousin sort of uncle. Great, isn't it?"

"Say that and keep smiling when there's a screaming baby around," Helen said, flicking him with a tea towel.

"I will. I promise," he said. "Because I mean it."

The teasing note had quite gone from his voice.

"You may not think it to look at him," Helen said to Polly, "but this six-foot-two hunk of masculinity is chief midwife and nursemaid for our livestock. Spoils 'em rotten. And he's putty in the little paws or hoofs of anything young and helpless. Heaven knows what he'll be like with a real live baby to fuss over."

Leon scowled. "I'll be perfectly sensible."

Polly was fascinated to see that he actually looked embarrassed. So he had his vulnerable – and, she had to confess, human – points after all.

Helen chuckled. "He'll be a devoted babysitter, I'm sure of that."

"So why all this talk of leaving?" he said, directing the conversation to safer ground. "You're both happy here. I don't know what I'd do without you."

"No problem at the moment. As things are, it'd take wild horses to drag me away. But suppose you took it into your head to marry someone like that girl you brought here before Christmas? Karen."

He frowned, shook his head. "No thanks."

"Why not? She's a nice girl – intelligent, independent, witty, not to mention glamorous – perfectly suited to you in every way, but not someone I could ever feel close to. I know that we couldn't live under the same roof for more than a weekend visit. I'm sure she feels the same way about me. We'd be at each other's throats in no time."

"I'm not going to marry Karen Hill," he said firmly. "She's just someone I happen to meet at the studios from time to time."

"Don't kid yourself, love." Helen winked at Polly. "She's got other ideas, like fancying her chances as the second Mrs Hammond. And to my mind she looks like a girl who knows what she wants and goes for it."

"Get on with loading the dishwasher, woman," Leon growled, "and stop organising my private life."

Karen Hill's face swam into Polly's dreams that night. In the silly way of dreams, Aunt Hester and Karen were organising the removal of Old Radbourne's mullioned windows and replacing them with double-glazed patio doors. Karen stared blankly at Polly who was struggling through heaps of slippery negatives in order to stop them.

The Glass Case

"It's for the best," Karen insisted. "So convenient."

She turned from Polly and drifted away on Leon's arm to wave Aunt Hester off on a cruise liner.

"But the windows!" Polly cried. "It's criminal to change them."

Leon smiled at her pityingly from the deck of the cruise liner. "You wouldn't have dared, would you? Karen has all the right ideas."

She awoke bristling with indignation, which rapidly turned to laughter as she realised the daftness of the dream. Odd though, she thought sleepily, she still seemed to hear the hiss of the ocean. She blinked herself properly awake and looked at the clock. Time she was getting up anyway and that sound was clearly nothing to do with the sea, but with the paws of a certain animal on the wood of the door.

She threw back the covers and went to let in Sam who woofed excitedly and covered her with enthusiastic licks. She backed off, laughing, and ordered him to sit on the rug while she bathed and dressed. He accompanied her downstairs and then sat gazing at her while she made toast and coffee in the empty kitchen. Helen appeared briefly, with a wan face, to explain that she couldn't face food these mornings and Leon had asked if Polly could make her own way down to meet the vet later.

"The men have their hands full. There's been a bit of trouble in the night, apparently," she said before she hastily retreated from the smell of coffee. "Prowlers – vandals or something. They're having to clear up something of a mess."

Polly hurried out after a quick breakfast and found Paul piling stones back on to the low wall behind the barn.

"This is the only wall that's suffered damage," he

159

answered at her anxious enquiry. "The intruders have been in the shed where we keep the animal feed, though. Done no more than open bags and shift things around. Nothing's actually been taken as far as we can see. Leon's checking round at the moment. The livestock's okay, thank goodness." He shook his head. "We don't get much vandalism round here as a rule. I can't understand it."

"Children from the village?" Polly suggested.

"I doubt it. They're welcome to come up here whenever they want to. No need to sneak about at night. Leon's always made a policy of encouraging the local children to take an interest. Quite a few of them help out here in their spare time."

"It's a wonder Sam didn't bark if there were prowlers about," Polly said, watching him snuffling among the long dead grasses banked up by the wall.

"Some guard dog he is." Paul snorted affectionately. "Soppy animal. He'd probably hold the torch for a burglar and think it was an interesting diversion in the boring hours when there's no one around to fuss over him. No, I mustn't be unkind to the poor old boy. He sleeps in the kitchen, which is over on the other side of the house. I doubt he'd hear anything." He wedged another stone into the gap. "The vet's here, by the way, if you want to make a start. Leon took your lights down. He'll look in later."

Mr MacKenzie, a blunt Scotsman, was in the clinic, a clean, neat room behind the pens. He was examining a kestrel that had been shot with an airgun when Polly joined him.

"Fit for transfer," he said as Polly set up her camera. "He'll be going to a centre that specialises in the care and rehabilitation of birds of prey. Next, I think we'll deal with the swan brought in a couple of days ago. It

160

had an unfortunate encounter with a power cable. Not squeamish are you? It's not a pleasant sight."

Squeamish or not, Polly had to get on with the job. She felt saddened at the accidental injuries and sickened by the mindless acts of cruelty that had been inflicted on some of the birds and animals. But she kept her feelings to herself, as did Mr MacKenzie as he continued his inspection and treatment. There was no time for sentiment. She had to record as much as she could.

Leon slipped in halfway through the session. Sometimes he quietly asked Polly to take a particular shot or helped to hold a patient who proved tetchy and inclined to peck or bite. His big hands were gentle and he seemed to have a remarkable rapport with these wild creatures, perhaps born of his intense desire to help them. They seemed to respond to his concern with quiet trust.

An atmosphere of intimacy built up in the small room, the three of them going about their individual tasks calmly and competently. It was almost a shock to Polly when Mr Mackenzie washed his hands after completing the final dressing, refused the offer of coffee because he'd a lot of calls to make, and went off to his car.

"Leave your stuff here," Leon said. He grimaced. "Better lock everything up. I suppose we'll have to be a bit more careful until we've caught the trespassers. However, work's over for the morning," he added firmly. "Time for those violets I promised you."

The breeze was soft against her face and there was real warmth in the sun. She followed Leon down a narrow track that ran by the high walls of the old kitchen garden. Beyond the garden the track merged with a grassy bridle path.

"This goes right down to the cliffs," he explained

as they strolled between leafless thickets of hazel and blackthorn. "Maybe tomorrow we could walk all the way. Takes a couple of hours there and back."

"I'm here to work, Leon," she pointed out.

"You're working for me and with me," he said solemnly. "And I'm perfectly willing to give you time off for good behaviour."

"Thanks a bunch," she said crisply, "but if I take on an assignment, I don't waste my client's time and money. Or my own." She concentrated on Sam bounding happily from side to side of the path, unwilling to meet the amused blue eyes that were fixed unwaveringly on her face.

"Very laudable," Leon said, clapping his gloved hands together in mock applause. "But think what you'd be missing: a guided walk through some of the loveliest country in England, a view at the end of it that'll knock your eyes out, maybe even a scramble down to the beach."

"No thanks," she said, not allowing herself to dwell on the tempting picture he painted.

He sighed. "You're a hard woman to please."

"My plan is to work tomorrow morning and early afternoon, then set off for home before it starts to get dark," she said. "If I get a good batch of photographs out of these two days, that's all the pleasing I need."

"You know what they say about all work and no play," he said softly.

"I'm here to do a job and I intend to do it properly. If you think that makes me dull, tough."

"But you're not dull. You only try to be."

She swung round to face him angrily.

"Why do we always have to get on to the subject of my so-called shortcomings?"

"Would you prefer to talk about me?"

"No thanks!"

He laughed. "That's better."

"What is?"

"The light of battle in your eyes. Makes me feel that the glass case is near to shattering."

She clenched her fists. It was hard to resist the urge to punch him on the nose. "I don't understand why on earth you have set yourself to antagonise me."

"Don't you? Perhaps it's because you've intrigued me since the first day we met."

"Why?"

He tipped his head on one side, regarding her thoughtfully. "I've asked myself that question more than once. It's a mystery. You're a mystery, Polly Burton, and, like the elephant's child, I have an insatiable curiosity."

"But I'm perfectly ordinary."

"That's where we must disagree."

Their footsteps had slowed. Now he caught her arm. She stared up into his eyes. Sun slanted through the leafless branches, catching them in a filmy, golden spotlight. His eyes were narrowed against the light and there was no laughter in his dark, bony face.

"You intrigue me, Polly, because there's a sadness about you that haunts me."

"What rubbish." She tried to shake her arm free but his grip was too strong.

"Won't you admit your fear, even to yourself?"

"There's nothing to admit."

"You'll not be a whole person until you face up to whatever it is that's bugging you. Or a happy one."

A blackbird flew up, chattering in alarm, from a bramble thicket. Somewhere distant a pheasant called raucously.

163

Polly barely noticed. She was aware of nothing but his eyes burning into hers, the mesmerising cadences of his voice, the hard grip of his fingers on her arm. And aware too of a deep persistent ache within, a strange sort of yearning weakness: something that responded to his touch, his voice, something that wanted to let go and lean against him and be comforted, something childlike, vulnerable.

Only she wasn't a child. And she wasn't in the least vulnerable to his professional charm.

He smiled gently. "Take a deep breath."

"I'm breathing perfectly satisfactorily, thank you." She regained control and snatched her arm away.

"Can't you smell the violets? After all, that's why I brought you here."

The faint, tantalising fragrance curled about them like the softest caress.

"There," he said, pointing.

The leaves spread in a thick green mass among the knobby blackthorn roots. He crouched down, parting the leaves to reveal the flower stems with their heavy-headed, purple-tipped buds.

"Not many fully-out yet and don't expect me to pick you a bunch. It's against my principles."

"Far better to leave them here for other people to enjoy," she agreed. She bent down to inspect them closer, reaching out a finger to touch the delicate flowers.

"Simple, perfect, unshowy," he said softly. "What could be better?"

"But I thought you were a man who liked big, brassy flowers like strelitzias?" The words were out before she could stop them. He looked puzzled. "You remember. You sent me this big arrangement when we were in South Africa."

"I did?"

"You did."

"I don't quite—"

"Big orange beaky things. Beloved of flower arrangers."

"I sent you those?" He frowned. "No I didn't, that damned receptionist did. I had to leave it to her. I couldn't hang about, I was running late. You didn't like them."

"Not my favourite flower."

"Nor mine," he said, grinning. "Sorry."

She felt oddly pleased that it hadn't been his choice, but she didn't want him to see that. She looked again at the violets, sniffing appreciatively at the scented air.

"They're beautiful. Makes you feel spring can't be too far off."

"Yep. And they hide their beauty away under their leaves, just like some people I could name" – he glanced sideways at her – "who hide behind frumpy clothes and prim expressions."

"Don't start again," she groaned. She straightened up. "Look, get off my back. I don't care what you think, so just keep your opinions to yourself."

She began to walk back the way they had come. It did nothing for her composure to hear him laughing.

"Don't think you can run away," he called after her. "Because I'm bigger than you, I've got longer legs and I'll always catch you up."

"Get lost!" she called back. But the breeze caught her words and tossed them heedlessly towards the fragile blue arch of the sky.

Helen and Paul went to visit friends in Dorchester after lunch, Polly spent the afternoon photographing the intricate plasterwork in the formal drawing room, a slow and painstaking business. Leon had taken himself off into his study and only when his voice behind her called, "Ready for something to eat?" did she realise how the hours had flown.

She climbed down stiffly from the stepladder and busied herself packing away her lights and reflectors.

"You'll have to put up with my undiluted company," he said. "Helen and Paul have rung to say they're staying out for dinner."

Polly wondered if she could plead a headache and retire with a book to her room.

"I'm not too bad a cook," he declared. "How does poached salmon in my special herb and wine sauce grab you? Followed by lemon soufflé and maybe a chunk of Stilton?"

She realised she was ravenous. She'd had no more than a quick sandwich at lunchtime and that seemed a long time ago. She decided against fleeing to her bedroom.

"Sounds great," she said, tastebuds already a quiver, and hoping he wasn't shooting her a line about his cooking.

They ate in the kitchen where he'd stuck candles in the necks of old wine bottles and thrown a gingham cloth over the scrubbed table.

"Our very own private bistro," he said, putting a plate of salmon accompanied by stir-fried vegetables down in front of her with a flourish. "Now try that and tell me if it isn't pretty good."

She was prepared to be disappointed. But she wasn't. Even better, the lemon soufflé, accompanied by a dish of thick yellow cream, was mouth-wateringly scrumptious.

"I've never known anyone refuse a second helping,"

he said, scraping the dish and piling it on her plate, "so I'm not even going to ask."

"I have to hand it to you," she said scooping up a spoonful of the soufflé, "you're no mean shakes in the culinary department. You could always set up in the restaurant business if you ever find yourself short of funds."

"Cooking for two, not forty-two, is more my scene. And I confess I only have a limited repertoire. I'm not up to Helen's standard. Not at all."

She wondered how many other girls had sat here being impressed by his culinary skills. But she was too sleepily full and content to give it more than a passing thought.

They sat chatting over coffee. The evening had passed effortlessly and he had been the perfect, attentive host. He hadn't teased her or needled her and she'd been content to let the conversation drift along in an easy unforced way.

He told her about his family. The father he scarcely remembered, his mother who had remarried and lived in Australia. "We get together once or twice a year, and occasionally I organise a reunion with my grandparents and any other relatives who care to join us. My ma's parents live out in Florida. They call it God's waiting room," he said, with a guffaw. "But if I'm as hale and hearty as they are in my eighties I'll be well pleased. My dad's father remarried after my grandmother died. He's gone now but he had a second big family, so I've several uncles and aunts and cousins from that union. Quite a rumbustious gathering when we all get together."

She felt a pang of envy. She'd hardly known her parents, let alone her grandparents who'd been dead by the time she was old enough to know about such things.

Her father had been an only child. Aunt Hester was her only blood relative, and she had no children.

"You're like Kate, my assistant. She has a big extended family. There've been so many divorces and remarriages, I don't know how she remembers all the names." She smiled, adding lightly, "I don't even have a cousin to call my own."

"Just count your blessings," he joked. "Christmas and birthdays are a nightmare." But the look he gave her was gentle and understanding.

She glanced away. She had no illusions. He'd turned on the charm specially. As he'd doubtless done dozens of times before with other girls. Karen Hill? Had she been given the full Hammond charm treatment?

She studied his profile as he made a fresh pot of coffee. He was whistling softly to himself. He looked relaxed and happy. Pity to shatter the companionable atmosphere that filled the kitchen as completely as the gentle warmth from the Aga, but she had to. They were alone and wouldn't be disturbed. It was a perfect opportunity to return the unwanted Christmas present.

He came back to the table with the coffee, surprised to see that she was on her feet and reaching for the torch on the dresser.

"Won't be a tick," she said. "There's something I want to fetch from the car. I'd almost forgotten about it."

There was no moon and clouds streamed across the glittering points of the stars as she went across the cobbled yard. The garage was a converted stable block, her old car housed at the far end. One of the double doors was flapping to and fro in the rising wind. She pulled it back, flicked her torch over the empty space where Paul's four-wheel drive usually sat, then went inside to open the boot of her own car.

She took out the gold box, leaving it on the roof of the car while she closed the boot. Then she froze.

A noise. A soft, shuffling, whispering noise. For a skin-prickling instant her thoughts went wildly to Kate's prophecies of clanking ghostly visitors. Then she grinned to herself. An animal. A mouse, a country rat maybe, or one of the cats she'd seen around. The mouse or the cat she didn't mind but he didn't quite fancy encountering the rat. She flashed the torch round to the far end of the garage. Eyes glittered in the beam, an arm jerked up to shield a face from the dazzle.

There was someone in the garage with her!

At that moment the wind caught the garage door and swung it shut with a crash. It caught her elbow and the torch jolted from her hand and smashed to the floor. She wanted to scream but her throat had gone harsh and dry. Shock held her rooted. The inky darkness closed in, suffocating – a thick, smothering blanket.

The door. She had to get it open. She had to find light . . . people. Leon! Did she cry his name aloud, or was it her mind shrieking in silent panic?

Voices. More than one! Coming nearer. Closing in on her.

She stepped backwards, her foot kicking the dropped torch, sending it clattering away.

Footsteps. Quiet footsteps moving towards her in the dark, bringing violence . . . evil . . . terror.

The nightmare burst over her. A living, waking night-mare, because she wasn't asleep but brutally, horribly awake.

Through her mind poured images of fear: raised hands,

dark, laughing, evil faces . . . No suppressing it now. Not a sensible thought in her head to drive the demons back. All was chaos, terror, blind mind-swamping panic.

A hand fingered her skirt, grabbed it, tugging . . .

All control went.

She screamed, the sound tearing out of her lungs, her throat. She put her hands over her face, but the screaming went on and on.

Then light flared as the naked overhead neon strip flickered and steadied. Another voice.

"What the devil . . . ?"

And his arms, Leon's arms, were around her, holding her, cradling her against the horror

"It's all right," he whispered, stroking her hair. "It's all right, sweetheart. You're safe. I'm here."

She went limp against him, blotting out everything except the knowledge that she was safe, that no harm could come to her while Leon held her close.

She was aware with the periphery of her mind that he was yelling. Not at her. At somebody else. She allowed her eyes to open a crack. Two boys. One no more than ten or eleven, the other gawkily in his early teens. They were cowering back against the onslaught of Leon's wrath, the younger one tearfully protesting, "We've done nothing bad. Honest. We were just mucking about."

And, like a play unfolding, a play in which she had no part and was merely an onlooker, they went back into the house, to the warm kitchen. She sat where Leon gently placed her in a chair by the Aga, a rug wrapped about her as though she were an invalid. The two boys trailed in miserably. She was aware that Leon gave them a stern dressing down before she closed her eyes and let the warmth soak into her icy limbs. When she opened them again, the boys were both sitting down drinking out of coffee mugs and munching biscuits. Leon was on the phone. Another blank interval. Then the sound of a car and another stranger, a man, was bending over her to apologise, shaking hands with Leon and going away again with the two boys in tow.

"Only a couple of mischievous kids," Leon said quietly. "They sneaked out when their parents thought they were in bed. Their father's just moved with his firm to Dorchester. They're in a rented cottage in the village. City kids. The countryside's one big adventure at the moment." He smiled wryly. "They got rather more in the way of excitement than they bargained for tonight. I reckon you put the fear of God into them. Their father'll do the rest."

She wanted to speak but all she could do was stare at him.

"Come on," he said. "We'll go into the sitting room."

He drew her to her feet, put his arms round her, half carrying her. Her legs moved slowly. It took an enormous effort to put one foot in front of the other. She knew that if he let go she would crumple to the floor, boneless as a rag doll.

She caught a glimpse of her reflection in a mirror in the hall. Was that really her? Eyes huge in a face the colour of ash. Must be. Sam rose yawning from the rug in front of the newly-banked log fire in the sitting room.

"Some guard dog you are," Leon scolded as the dog wound himself around them. She felt his tail thumping against her legs. "Slept through everything, wretched animal."

Sam licked Polly's hand as though in apology. She wanted to smile, but her face refused. Would she ever

171

be able to smile again if the mad swirls of colour and fear continued to surge in her mind?

Now she was sitting on the deep, comfortable couch. Leon was beside her, holding her trembling hands in his, drawing her round to face him.

"Look at me, Polly," he said quietly.

She lifted her heavy lashes, fixed her eyes on his.

"Good girl." Then, slowly and clearly, he said, "There's nothing to be afraid of. You're safe. You've had a shock. It brought back memories you've been trying to suppress for most of your life."

She swallowed. "No . . . no, it's not . . ." she croaked.

"Stop it, Polly." His grip was warm and hard on her cold hands. "Stop trying to deny it happened. You've bottled everything up for far too long. You wouldn't even tell your Aunt Hester . . . Oh, yes, she and I have had some interesting conversations. She said you would never speak of what you saw to anyone. Not to doctors or counsellors. Not to your friends. Not to her."

She tried to drag her hands out of his, but his fingers bit into hers fiercely.

"Nothing . . . nothing to tell . . ."

"Can't you see that you're only making it worse? If you go on petending, go on hugging the fear to yourself, you'll never be free of it. It'll return again and again to haunt you." Firelight flickered over his face, kindled the blue eyes to a warmth that touched the shivering depths of her fear. "You can't go on living half a life," he whispered.

"I'm not . . ."

"What were you, eight, nine, that spring when you went to visit your parents?" His voice was implacable, cruel. "They were working on a dig in North Africa. There were mountains, an isolated valley. You remember that, don't you? The dry sandy valley, the arid, ridged mountains. You remember the emptiness, the isolation. Tell me how it was. Tell me what you saw. Tell me about your parents."

As he spoke the pictures were in her head. She was there, a sturdy little girl in blue shorts, a blue bow on her ponytail. Her father, so tall and strong, holding her hand and smiling. A feeling of great contentment. Her mother . . .

"My . . . my mother." Her voice was thick and hoarse. "I . . . I remember how . . . how her hair looked in the sunlight."

"Yes?"

"It was red gold, lighter than Aunt Hester's. She wore it long and loose. It seemed to hold the sun. I thought it was so beautiful. I wished my hair was like that . . ." Her voice trailed away.

"Go on," he said softly.

"They loved each other, she and my father. Those men . . ." She broke off. "I can't, I can't," she whispered.

"You can. There were three of them, tribesmen, intent on wreaking vengeance because they hadn't been hired to help with the dig. They got high on booze and drugs and went crazy."

"Stop! Please stop!" she begged.

Leon released her hands, took her by the shoulders and shook her roughly.

"Polly, go on! Tell me what you saw that night in the house."

She couldn't take her eyes off his.

"Don't make me, Leon."

"It's for your own sake, love," he said, gentle now. His grip eased on her shoulders. His fingers moved

173

to her neck, traced the line of her jaw with butterfly delicacy, pushed back the clinging tendrils of hair from her cheek.

And perhaps it was the tenderness in his touch that finally cracked the iron-hard dam of her control, allowing the welter of suppressed emotion to sweep aside the last crumbling vestiges of the barrier behind which she had sheltered for so long.

The story poured out of her. She dug deep, drawing up pictures she had buried for years, spilling them in their raw technicolour horror into images that made her cover her face with her hands, as if – impossibly – to blot them out.

She stumbled over the words. In broken phrases she spoke of how she had woken from sleep when she'd heard shouts from the other room. How she'd scrambled to the door, opened it on to the spartan living room. The men were there, in a mass of tumbled furniture and overturned lamps. Her father cried out and was silenced, kicked aside. The men's shadows leapt high on the rough white walls, their clawed hands holding knives. Their shouts beat in her ears and drowned out her mother's diminishing screams.

She'd shrunk back, dumb with shock, and when they spied her their hands reached out for the small helpless figure in the pink nightie. She saw the gleam of their teeth in their livid faces, the glint of their mad eyes, the blood that spattered their robes, before they were dragged away by the rescuers who had burst in to save her from the fate her parents had shared.

She was sobbing now, sobbing as she had never done all those years ago. As she'd never done since. She knew she was making a great soggy patch on Leon's black sweater, but there was no way she could stop. It was as though all the bottled up horror of her childhood was pouring out of her in one cataclysmic storm of weeping.

Leon held her tight and close, his hand stroking her hair in long, slow sweeps. After a while she became aware of it and, sensing some change in her, the hand paused, removed itself and returned with a large white handkerchief.

She mopped her eyes, blew her nose and tried with partial success to control the uneven shuddering of her breathing.

"I'm . . . I'm sorry," she began. "I've never . . . I don't usually—"

"Shh." His fingers touched her lips, silencing her. "There's only one way to tackle fear, Polly," he murmured, "and that's to face it. Brave girl, you've done that. Nothing, I promise you, will ever seem as bad again."

She gave a little sigh and leaned against him, lids drooping in sudden exhaustion over her tear-swollen eyes. She must look a wreck, she thought faintly, but somehow it didn't seem to matter. All that did matter was the golden glow from the fire, the beat of his heart beneath her cheek, the comforting arms. She felt dreadfully sleepy, drowning in langour, not the undermining weakness of shock, but an almost sensual relaxation of body and mind.

Perhaps she dozed, perhaps she just rested within the circle of Leon's arms as they both stared peacefully into the glowing heart of the fire and shared the drowsy moments of silence. He seemed to have become someone she had known all her life. Being here in his arms was the most natural thing in the world.

Her thoughts ebbed and flowed, like a drifting, lazy tide. They kept coming back to Leon, reminding her that this was the man she had both resented and disliked. Yet

175

this was the person she had poured out her heart to in a way that had never been possible before. She could hardly believe it. The whole series of events had the quality of a dream.

She stirred and glanced up at his face through still-damp lashes. It was true enough. It had happened. She was here.

"Hi there," he said. He was watching her, his blue eyes warm with an emotion she couldn't read. "I thought you'd nodded off."

"I nearly did," she confessed.

She should be feeling embarrassed or uncomfortable, shouldn't she? She was alone in the house, curled up on a couch with a man she claimed to detest, with only a dopey dog snoring on the hearthrug as chaperon. She should be pushing herself out of his embrace, making it clear she appreciated his kindness and concern, but would prefer their relationship back on a formal footing. She didn't want to give the impression that the shock which had prompted her stupid outburst was to be taken as a sign that she was vulnerable to his charms.

But she didn't want to move. None of these perfectly sound arguments seemed to have any bearing on her immediate needs, nor to have any connection with her resolution to get away from him.

His arms tightened about her. Her hands, somehow, found themselves sliding up his black sweater, moving round so that her fingers met at the back of his neck. His lips touched her forehead. Her fingers wound into the rough, curling hair at the nape of his neck. His mouth moved to her mouth, her body leant into his, her lips parted. His breathing quickened, hers matched it. His hands ran the length of her spine. Every nerve end leapt

176

to quivering attention. She dug her fingers into the hard muscles of his shoulders.

"Oh, Polly, my darling," he breathed.

She sighed against his mouth. "Oh, Leon."

"Oh, blast and damnation!"

"What?" she said breathlessly.

He released her abruptly. "I'd better answer the damn thing."

She realised that the phone in the hall was ringing. Had been ringing persistently for the last half-minute.

He got up. "Back in a minute. Don't go away."

He strode off, muttering under his breath.

Polly sat there, eyes half closed. She smiled. She felt it to be a soppy, foolish smile. What must she look like, sitting all by herself smiling like a Cheshire cat . . .

She jerked bolt upright. For God's sake, what was she thinking of?

She looked round as though seeing the room for the first time. Sam eyed her from the rug, flapped his tail in acknowledgement, closed his eyes again and returned to chasing dream rabbits, paws twitching.

She'd been dreaming too. She'd been on the point of . . . No, she hadn't!

She felt a wash of heat in her face as she smoothed down the creases in her skirt, ran her hands over her tousled hair. It was the after-affects of the emotional switchback she'd been on this evening. He'd taken advantage of a moment of weakness on her part. She summoned up indignation and mixed it with guilty thoughts of Charles. Funny, though, it was hard at this minute to recall Charles's face clearly. But it was easy enough to imagine his dismay and despair at her thoughtless, treacherous behaviour with Leon.

Leon. She looked at the crumpled cushions. Had he

snuggled down on this very couch with Karen Hill? Not to mention all those other, willing girls who'd fancied him.

Well, she wasn't one of them.

She jumped to her feet, tugging down her shirt. He was a wolf! Only it hadn't seemed like that a few moments ago. It had seemed . . . No, no . . . How could she have let herself go like that? Uncaring of everything except the blissful, sensuous contact of their bodies.

Blissful?

Pure imagination. Thank heaven for the phone. Saved by the bell. Literally. *Charles, Charles, I didn't mean it. I'm so sorry.*

When Leon came back into the room she was poised for flight, her fingers turning the engagement ring on her finger, her smile bright and fixed. She would make her excuses now, plead exhaustion and go to her room.

But as he came towards her, tall, muscular, dark hair untidy above his eyebrows, all her resolve melted.

He held out his hands, smiling, and more than anything she wanted to put hers into them. She clutched her ring, as a drowning sailor clutches at a lifebelt.

"I . . . I think I'd better . . ." she began, then heard the sound of a car on the gravel outside. Helen and Paul returning.

Leon groaned. "We're doomed to be interrupted."

She should have been delighted, not overwhelmed by a wave of disappointment.

"The phone call was from someone I was to have met on Wednesday," Leon explained. "Only he's had an unexpected call to New York. Which means I'll have to drive up to Edinburgh early tomorrow to catch him before he goes." He moved towards her, kissed her lightly on her lips, his arms sliding round her waist. "Sorry, sweetheart, but this rather wrecks the weekend, and I've got a packed schedule next week with this series I'm getting together on backyard conservation." He looked quite devastated at the prospect. A clever ploy, she told herself. He'd probably had plenty of practice. "Then the following week I'm tied up with this Jersey Conference."

"I'll be busy, too," she interrupted brightly.

"I'll ring you—"

"No need," she said. "I can contact Helen and Paul about future visits."

He frowned. "But—"

"I'll send on the proofs as soon as they're ready. When did you say you wanted everything completed – April? I can probably fit in a couple more visits between now and then. That should give you plenty of material to work on."

"Polly, I . . ."

She took his hands and removed them from her waist. She took a step backwards. Standing so close to him seemed to have an odd effect on her breathing.

"I do appreciate your kindness to me tonight."

"Kindness? Kindness be damned!" He seemed genuinely distraught. Good acting. Good acting, that was all, she thought desperately. "Polly, I thought—"

"An Easter deadline will suit me fine." She had to keep on talking. Either that or lose all sense of proportion and succumb to this knee-weakening urge to melt back into his arms. "I'll be getting married then, did I mention it?"

"No!"

"Portugal," she rushed on. "That's where we're spending our honeymoon. It's all booked. A friend of Charles has this villa he's not using . . . Oh, hello there." Mercifully, Paul and Helen were coming into the room, casting

179

off coats and scarves. Rescuing her. She smiled at them brilliantly. "Had a good evening? We've been having fun and games here. The vandals have been revealed. Leon will tell you all about it."

Still wearing the same false smile, she walked across the room to the door. "If you'll excuse me now, I'm absolutely dead on my feet. 'Night all."

It took a supreme effort of will not to run out of the room before she changed her mind, which was, all of a sudden, a muddle of contradictory impulses. Half of her wanted to stay. The other half wanted to run far, far away and hide.

She didn't sleep too well. The creaks and bumps of an old house settling for the night infiltrated her uneasy dreams. Then it wasn't just the house but the sound of a car outside.

It was still dark. She got out of bed and crept like a thief to the window, carefully drawing back the curtain a fraction.

Down below was Leon's silver Jag. He was putting a case in the boot, his face and body illuminated in the light spilling from the front door. He pulled down the boot lid, paused, glanced towards her window.

Could he see her? No, impossible. Yet he lifted his hand in a half wave, almost as though he sensed her watching. Then he walked back to the house, switched off the lights, pulled the door closed with a heavy thunk. His footsteps scrunched across the gravel, the interior car light outlined him briefly as he slid into the driver's seat, then the car was moving down the drive, disappearing into the darkness. A last flickering reflection of its headlights as it drove up the steep lane towards the village, then it, and Leon, were gone.

She went back to bed and threw herself among the tangled bedclothes.

She was rid of him. She could have a whole relaxed day to herself before driving back to London. She wouldn't have to worry about bumping into Leon round every corner. That was good, wasn't it?

So why did she feel so miserable?

She'd be able to concentrate on her photography with nobody to engage her in awkward conversation. Nobody to tease and ruffle her feathers.

Nobody to kiss her with a passion that melted her bones.

She jolted upright in bed, eyes wide and alarmed. What madness was coming over her?

"Leon." She breathed his name aloud into the darkness. The sound seemed to brush against her lips like a caress. Her hand flew to her mouth as though to erase the sensation, but there was no wiping it away. No rubbing out the sense of desolation that welled up at the thought of him speeding away from her.

She hugged her knees. Made herself deliberately think of Karen Hill, of the other, faceless, girls who'd been in his life. Girls he'd perhaps brought here or to his riverside flat. Casual liaisons. No reason to suppose he saw her other than just another scalp for his belt. Love 'em and leave 'em. That had been his policy for years. Maybe it gave extra spice to his pursuit to know that she, Polly, was engaged to someone else. A thoroughly worthy and reliable man, not a rich, spoiled charmer.

She tried to conjure up Charles's image, but those teasing blue eyes, that other face superimposed itself, blotting out everything she had considered secure and unchangeable, emphasising one overwhelming unpalatable fact.

Somehow, against her will and her reason, she had become irresistibly attracted to a man she wanted to despise.

Seven

It was an infection, she told herself firmly, like measles. His charm had acted like a virus, taking hold while she was temporarily off guard. Now it had to be treated with clinical care: isolation from the source of the infection, a hefty dose of common sense, the careful nurturing of antidotes in the form of a caring fiancé and concentration on work.

By daylight rain was sluicing down and even when it stopped in mid-morning the raw, damp cold did nothing to snap her out of the gloomy mood into which she'd sunk.

It was difficult to concentrate. Her mind was inclined to wander down impossible alleyways where the prescribed common sense had no effect at all. Every stone of the house, every tree she passed in the grounds, every bird and animal in the hospital, seemed to speak of Leon.

A distant figure striding across a windswept field made the breath catch in her throat. An unexpected footstep made her spin round eagerly, and when it was only Paul or Helen the fluttering butterflies in her stomach turned leaden and earthbound.

It was no use, she'd not be sensible – herself again – until she left Old Radbourne. This was his territory. His character was inextricably bound up in the place. Once she got away she'd be okay.

She left soon after lunch. Helen gave her a warm hug.

"Come again soon," she said. "It's been lovely having you here." She paused, then said gently, "I'm so sorry you had such an upsetting experience last evening."

How much had Leon told them? She'd smiled and dismissed the incident.

"Just my bad luck," she said. "And at least you found out who the trespassers were. Nothing too serious, thank goodness."

"A shock for you, nevertheless."

"At the time, yes. No ill effects today, though."

She thought about that as she walked to the garage. And it was true. She didn't doubt that those appalling images from her past would from time to time raise their ugly heads. The ache of loss whenever she thought about her parents was certainly still there. Perhaps it always would be. But the shock of last night's events, the outpouring of grief, had triggered some adjustment in her mind, her emotions. She wasn't quite sure what. There was a sense of . . . well, not quite release – it was far too soon and the memories went too deep – but there was a difference, a tiny element of calm had been introduced. Whether it would grow and spread to overcome the maelstrom of remembered trauma, remained to be seen. But at least, she thought with surprise, she was actually reviewing it with an objectivity that had been impossible before. A small step, but a hopeful one.

Paul had gone ahead to carry her gear to the car. The garage doors stood wide open and the sound of his cheerful whistle came to meet her. No nasty dark shadows to frighten her into hysterics today. She sensed that Paul had arranged it like this, in case she took fright again. What a nice couple Paul and Helen were. For their

184

sake she hoped Leon didn't marry Karen Hill. Then she sighed. It was none of her business. Why should she care? But she did. For Helen and Paul, for the house, for . . .

She almost went flying.

She'd edged round the car to the driver's seat and nearly tripped over the box containing the negligée. She'd forgotten all about it. She must have left it on the car roof and it had slithered off when she was crashing about in a panic. Now the box lay open on the floor, its contents spilling into a greasy puddle of rainwater that had seeped under the door.

Slowly she bent and picked it up. It had soaked up a great dirty splodge of water. The rest of it flowed over her hands, cool and sensuous, and she felt a desolate pang because Leon had given her this beautiful thing and it was ruined.

But she mustn't, *mustn't* think of him. She snatched up the negligée, stuffed it back in its box and threw it on to the back seat. Then she waved goodbye to Paul and reversed the car out of the garage.

At the top of the valley where the lane turned towards the village she stopped, switched off the engine and got out of the car with her camera.

She walked across to the field gate. She'd thought there might be a good shot from here, and there was. The manor huddled in the misty valley, trees and shrubs and lawns lapping at its walls like an eccentric garment. It looked snug, a haven, tranquil and timeless under the ragged, racing clouds. She felt that she had left a little piece of her heart there. It was the place where she had shared her secret unhappiness with Leon as so many people had confided their secrets, their dreams, their hopes, their fears down the centuries. And been comforted, as she had been.

She took her pictures, remembering the stories Leon had told her as he'd shown her round by candlelight on her first visit. And somehow, thinking of the long history of the house helped to put her own troubles into perspective.

She was in a more positive frame of mind as she drove to London through the louring grey afternoon. She turned her thoughts resolutely to the future. To Charles. She knew he was booked to play golf this afternoon. She'd give him a ring when she got back. Perhaps they could go out for a meal. They really should get down to organising the wedding, as they'd been promising themselves since before Christmas. It would be quiet. Neither of them wanted a big show. A few close friends for a wedding breakfast after a registry office ceremony. No fuss, no ostentation. Then the Portuguese honeymoon. Long, lazy, warm days. Romantic, pine-scented nights . . .

Her hands tightened on the wheel and she frowned into the gloom.

When she'd spoken to Charles, when the arrangements were finalised, she'd forget this silly business with Leon entirely.

Polly phoned Charles when she got home. He was still out. She left a message on his answerphone. She thought about trying his mobile but rejected the idea. She didn't want to interrupt him if he was still in the clubhouse having a meal and a drink with his golfing friends. Or perhaps he'd gone off with them somewhere to finish the evening. Whatever, she didn't want to bother him unnecessarily.

She replaced the receiver feeling vaguely let down, which was silly because Charles hadn't expected her to be home until late. She could hardly blame him for making alternative arrangements.

She mooched around the flat, unpacked her bag, switched on the radio and switched it off again, ran a bath, swooshed in an extravagant amount of bath oil and lit a couple of aromatherapy candles that promised scented relaxation. A long, hot soak would dispel the restlessness, then she'd have an early night.

The phone rang when she was half undressed. She leapt to answer it, flooded with relief. Charles! The evening was salvaged. She could make the bath a quick one and change to go out.

"Ah, you got home safely." That deep, familiar voice. Her stomach tightened and her heartbeat quickened, thumping so noisily that she wondered if it was audible in Edinburgh.

"Of course I did," she said loudly, to cover the sound. "Was there any reason why I shouldn't?"

"Flood, fire, pestilence. Any number of inconveniences."

"If you've anything of importance to tell me, will you please get on with it."

"This is a purely social call," he said amiably.

"Then would you mind not cluttering up the line? I'm expecting a genuinely important call." Well, it wasn't really a fib. Charles might get home any moment, switch on his answerphone and call her.

"Have you no sympathy for a poor bloke holed up in a hotel room with no one to talk to?"

"Hotels have bars," she said. "Bars have obliging barmaids who'll lend an ear to any sob story."

"It isn't a barmaid I'm in need of," he said softly. "It's you, my darling Polly."

She swallowed, said coldly, "Do stop it. I'm not an impressionable teenager who can be sweet-talked into . . . into . . ."

"Into what?"

"Into your bed!" she shouted. "There. Is that clear enough?"

"Perfectly." He chuckled. "But I wasn't thinking along those lines. At least, not quite."

"You were. Don't think you can pull the wool over my eyes, Leon Hammond. You may have lured Karen Hill or any number of other girls on to your casting couch, but I'm immune to your brand of seduction."

"Casting couch?" He sounded bemused. "This isn't Hollywood, love. And as for Karen, I've no designs on her. Never have had."

"Please Leon, I won't be one of your cheap conquests." There were tears in her eyes, though whether of anger or pain she couldn't tell. All she knew was that she had to get Leon off her back. Break his hold on her here and now, or she was lost. "Do you understand me, Leon? I won't be harrassed like this."

There was a long silence.

Then he said, his tone subtly altered, almost as though he found an uncharacteristic difficulty in finding the right words, "Did yesterday evening mean nothing to you, Polly?"

She made an effort to keep her voice steady.

"I'm grateful to you, Leon, very grateful. You were wonderfully supportive and understanding. I appreciate that. You were probably quite right. I had been bottling up a lot of bad memories and I'm only sorry that you had to suffer my childish outburst. I do apologise." She closed her eyes tight. "But just because I'm grateful, that doesn't mean I have any other sort of feeling for you." She forced herself to go on, word by painful word, amazed that her voice sounded so level, so cold. "I'm marrying Charles soon. I've no intention of wrecking my chances of a happy marriage with any sort of casual affair, with you or anyone else. So please stop playing your silly games. I don't appreciate them."

"I'm not playing games, Polly." There was an urgency now threading his words. "If I ask you one question, will you answer it honestly?"

She hesitated. "If I can."

"Are you in love with Charles?" There was a small, tense silence. "If the answer's yes, then I won't bother you again. If the answer's no, then wild horses wouldn't keep me away. Because you'll be making the biggest mistake of your life—"

She cut across his words. How could he know or understand the way Charles had been part of her life for so long? How could he know about the bonds of friendship and trust that bound her to him? How did Leon's failed marriage, his casual affairs, qualify him to give her advice?

"I love Charles," she said coldly and clearly.

Silence again on the line. She had to be the one to break it. She must break it, before her resolve weakened.

"I think it would be altogether more convenient if you found someone else to continue with the work at Old Radbourne."

"Polly, you can't mean it." His voice was harsh.

She didn't know if he was referring to what she'd said about Charles or Old Radbourne. But it didn't matter. It was immaterial.

189

"I do mean it. I'll get my assistant to send you a list of photographers that I can recommend as reliable."

"I see. If that's the way you want it."

"I do. And you'll keep your side of the bargain? Not to contact me again?"

"I wouldn't waste my time. Or yours," he said in a voice now so hard and icy that it made her shrivel inside.

"Goodbye, Leon."

He didn't answer. The phone went down with a crash at the other end.

She stood there motionless. Then, slowly, she began to look round at the familiar room: her room, in her own house. She thought of the office and darkroom downstairs, of the hard work that had gone into building her business and this little, private retreat. She waited for the usual lift of pleasure, of pride. But there was nothing. No comfort, no warmth. Nothing.

She walked back into the bathroom, finished undressing and got into the scented water of the bath. The candles flickered, sending their hopeful message of gentle relaxation.

It didn't work. No panacea of warmth or scent or light could remove the feeling of desolation. Or the overpowering sensation of loss and loneliness.

It wasn't Charles who rang first that evening, but Aunt Hester.

"Darling, I'll be in town for a little shopping later this week. Shall we meet for lunch on Saturday? Did you have a lovely Christmas? Mine was perfectly delightful." She laughed wickedly. "There was this divine Frenchman, a fellow guest. Absolutely charming and an accent to lure the birds from the trees. But he had to return to

190

his business in Cannes. And, I rather suspect, his wife. *C'est la vie*. And now I have to console myself with a little spending spree before I leave on my cruise. To have something pleasurable to look forward to is such a comfort when one's sensibilities are a trifle bruised . . ."

Aunt Hester's frivolous chatter did nothing to ease the dull ache that seemed to have settled under Polly's ribs. Nor did Charles's call later.

"Sorry I was out earlier. You were back sooner than you expected, weren't you? If I'd have known . . . well, I got caught up with other things. I've got that shopping mall contract pretty well tied up, by the way."

"Great," she said, trying to inject enthusiasm into her voice. "Sorry I couldn't help out."

"Not at all. It went very well." He paused, then said sounding a touch harassed, "I do have a tremendous amount to do this week. It'll be the weekend, I'm afraid, before I'll be clear to meet you."

"Oh, I was hoping . . . well, never mind." She managed a teasing laugh. "We still have plenty of time to talk about Easter, don't we? Though I think we shouldn't hang about too long."

"Easter?"

"The wedding." She swallowed hard. "I'm . . . I'm looking forward to Portugal."

"Yes, of course," he said. "We'll discuss it thoroughly then. I'll give you a call in the week and book *Mario's* for Friday night. Will seven thirty suit you?"

She put down the phone wishing that Charles had made their date sound like something other than a business appointment, that he had whispered sentimental nonsense in her ear, said that he loved her, wanted her – anything to warm the chilly deadness she felt inside, to brush away the tenacious cobwebs of melancholy.

Despite the relaxing bath she spent a restless night. She felt gritty-eyed and out of sorts to face the new week. For once, Kate's colourful brand of good humour failed to raise her spirits. She tried to respond to Kate's usual wisecracks as the days inched past on leaden feet, to put on a cheerful face, but it was an effort.

"I reckon there's a bad case of post-Christmas blues lurking in this office," Kate said one lunchtime as they sat in the office, delving into the foil containers she'd fetched from the Chinese takeaway up the road. "Want to talk about it?"

"Nothing to talk about," Polly said, concentrating on spearing a prawn among the fried rice.

"Pull the other one. You've mooched about in your own private, doomy black cloud all week." She frowned. "You and Charles had a tiff?"

"Of course not," Polly said stiffly.

"Pity." Kate sniffed. "A bit more action on that front might liven you up a bit."

"Don't talk rubbish."

"Then what?"

"Nothing. I've told you. What is this? You fancying yourself as an agony aunt or something? If so, forget it. I can manage my own affairs, thank you very much."

"So there is something."

Polly jabbed at another prawn. "Give it a rest," she muttered. "I'm not in the mood."

"Look, Poll, you can thump me on the nose for sticking my oar in, but I hate to see you looking like this. So I'm going to say my piece." Kate's impish face was serious. "It's weird, really. You've been to Dorset twice. Both times you've come back looking as though you've had the stuffing knocked out of you. What is it with that place?"

"Oh, didn't I tell you? Weird isn't the half of it. There I was on the A30, minding my own business and down came this beam of light and bingo! Next thing I knew I was on this spaceship with these giant green jellies . . ."

"At least your sense of humour hasn't totally deserted you." Kate leant across the desk, her stare unblinking. "Suppose I made an alternative suggestion. Like dropping a certain name into the conversation. Leon Hammond. Howzat?"

"How's what?" But to Polly's mortification she felt a hot tide of colour flood her face. She busied herself foraging for the last prawn.

Kate sat back and nodded judiciously. "I thought so. Come on. Tell Auntie Kate. You clearly need a shoulder to cry on, girl."

"I do not," Polly began, then faltered as she saw the sympathy in Kate's eyes. Wisecracks she could stand, sympathy unhinged her precarious composure. "Bit spicy this sweet and sour," she lied, groping for a tissue.

"As if," said Kate sardonically. "So, the delectable Leon's got you in a tizz, has he?"

"Not at all," she protested, blowing her nose into the tissue. "Well, in a sort of way. But it's not what you're thinking."

"What am I thinking?"

"You tell me."

"That you've fallen for him."

"No!"

Kate looked unconvinced. Polly began on a stammering denial, but somehow, with Kate – very quietly now –

putting in questions at the right moment, it turned into a full-blown saga. The whole story came out, right from that first meeting on the South African beach. Her thoughts, her feelings, her fear of him. "He's proved a pain in the neck from the first moment I saw him," she burst out at the end. "He's messing up my life and I wish to heaven I'd never clapped eyes on him."

"But you did. And now you're in love with him. Go on, admit it."

"I'm not! Whatever . . . feeling I have for him, it's only a silly passing fancy."

"Aha. Now we're getting close. Good grief, Poll, you may be God's gift to photography but when it comes to men you haven't a clue."

"It's Charles I want. It's Charles I love. It's Charles I'm going to marry."

"If you say that often enough you'll start to believe it."

"I do believe it. Because it's true," Polly bellowed, taking refuge in anger. She stood up and pushed her chair back so hard that it crashed against the wall. "I won't have my life – my future – mucked up by anyone. Particularly by a philandering know-all like *him*." She grabbed an empty foil container, screwed it up viciously and hurled it into the waste-paper basket. "I've got work to do and I'll be pleased if you'll get on with yours. There's nothing more to be said. The whole silly business is finished. Over. Kaput. I've told him to find another photographer. I've no intention of ever seeing him again. If you really want to help, instead of sitting there and pontificating about my love life—"

"Or lack of it."

—"then make out a list of half a dozen decent photo-graphers and post it to him with my bill. And stick on every extra that you can think of." She picked up her camera bag and stalked to the door, turning once to scowl at Kate. "And I don't want to hear his name mentioned again. Understand?"

"You're the boss," Kate said sweetly. "But I think you're making a big mistake."

Polly slammed the door.

She wished in the days that followed that she could slam the door so easily on her feelings. She did her best. She clung stubbornly to the thought that once she'd seen Charles everything would be all right again. Charles was her rock, her loyal, devoted fiancé. She couldn't imagine life without him.

But her resolution was constantly undermined by images of Leon.

She saw him a dozen times a day, and each time her heart gave the same treacherous lurch of joy before brutal reality intruded and the dark head glimpsed from the car, the pair of broad shoulders thrusting through a crowd could be seen to belong to some other man. She schooled herself to concentrate on driving or walking instead of glancing at passers-by.

Unfortunately, the forthcoming wildlife conference in Jersey was newsworthy. He was to be one of the speakers. Once or twice she opened a newspaper and didn't have time to shut it before she glimpsed a picture of him. Another time, she flicked open a magazine in search of an ad that contained one of her photographs and his name sprang out at her from a full page spread. She lifted a rug from the back seat of the car, and there was a photograph of him, with a tawny owl in his hands, that must have slipped from her folder.

It was as if some horrid fate had decided to punish her for allowing her emotions to get out of hand. As though it stood over her mocking, saying, 'This is what happens when you let your heart rule your head: confusion, pain, turmoil.'

Business, unfortunately, was slack. The Lawson crash had hit her harder than she cared to admit to Kate, or even to herself. She told herself she'd soon make up the deficit. She filled the gaps by visiting all her old contacts, tried a few new ones, and was met mostly with bland smiles and polite, vague promises to get in touch that undermined the confidence she usually felt in her work.

So it gave her quite a boost when Kate met her with some excitement as she walked into the office on Friday afternoon. A prospective client had been in touch.

"It's nothing definite, so don't get your hopes up too much," Kate said, "but I get the feeling that if you play your cards right, this could lead to big things."

"Even a few little ones would be welcome at this particular minute. Who is it? Some estate agent wanting mug shots of desirable properties for his leaflets?"

"Better. Mr Mahlen D. Moon the Second, no less."

"Who?"

Kate giggled, then said in a phoney Texan drawl, "Honey chile, I don't have much time in lil ole England, but I'd sho like to meet Miss Polly Burton."

"Gawd, what an accent. He'd have you up for wrongful impersonation if he could hear you. So what did he want?"

"You, Poll, to take happy-snaps of his latest acquisition. Or at least he might. He's bought a crumbling Welsh castle with the idea of fitting it out with all mod cons. Money no object, I gather. He read the book and liked what he saw.

It's just what we need. Someone with a private oilfield or two who lights fat cigars with dollar bills."

"That rich, eh?"

"Must be. He's off to Hawaii or somewhere next. Probably in search of an island paradise to buy. Anyway, I did rather gather you weren't the only photographer he was considering, so it'll have to be best bib and tucker and bags of sweet talk for you tomorrow."

"Tomorrow?"

"Two thirty sharp. At the Skyhigh Hotel, Heathrow. He can spare you ten minutes, I believe, for you to convince him that you're the one that he needs before he flies off into the wide blue yonder." She stared pointedly at Polly's dishevelled locks. "You can have your hair done in the morning."

"No time," Polly said. "I'm meeting Aunt Hester for lunch."

"I have this friend," Kate said, reaching for the phone and dialling before Polly realised what she was up to. "She owes me a favour. She'll fit you in early. She's got this very swish salon and she's a demon with the scissors."

"No. I can cut my own hair, thanks."

"What?" Kate shrieked. "To meet a Texan tycoon? You must be joking. Think of the glossy class of female he must be used to . . . That you, Vee? Kate here. I've got an urgent problem. You will be an angel and help out, won't you?"

Mario's on Friday night was packed to the doors, but Charles had secured his usual table in a quiet alcove screened by a bank of greenery. Polly scanned the menu, listened to the cheerful buzz of people enjoying themselves and wondered where her healthy appetite had gone.

197

She chose from the menu at random, hoping she'd be able to eat some of it, and concentrated on Charles's account of the deal he'd done. The words really didn't sink in but she nodded and made encouraging comments in the right places and kept her eyes fixed on his face, trying to etch it into her memory as though by sheer willpower that other, importunate image might be banished from her mind.

Kind, reliable Charles. She felt a warm surge of affection lap round the edges of the knot of confusion in her chest. He was so very dear to her. How could she possibly imagine that the distressing emotions that Leon roused in her were more important than what she had already? Impulsively, she reached out and laid her hand on his.

"It's so good to see you again," she said. "It seems ages since we were last together." She smiled shakily. "I've missed you."

"Have you, my dear?"

"I can't think how I'd ever manage without you," she said, meaning it. He'd always been there for her, a steady, reliable, calming influence. She appreciated such qualities more than ever at this moment.

His fine features quivered slightly. He cleared his throat. "I expect – I'd hope – that you'd manage very well. After all, you're an independent, modern young woman, with a promising career."

He carefully pulled his hand out from under hers as the waiter placed a fan of sliced melon surrounded by raspberry sauce in front of her.

"You're capable in every way," Charles declared firmly and turned his attention to his minestrone soup. When he'd taken a couple of mouthfuls and had carefully dabbed his mouth with a napkin, he leant back and said in his precise, careful tones, "That is why I feel what I have to say to you now – though it may surprise you at first – will be accepted in your usual sensible and level-headed fashion."

"Sensible? How do you mean?"

"Just this, my dear." His smile was cool, but there was a certain nervousness evident in the way his fingers crumpled the edge of the napkin. "I've always been deeply conscious of the age gap between us. It is something that has increasingly troubled me."

"But I don't give it any thought at all!"

He held up his hand. "Allow me to finish. There is another factor, which I shall come to in a moment, but for now I should like to say that, after careful consideration, I feel I must ask you to release me from our engagement."

She'd just speared a piece of melon. The fork fell to her plate with a clatter. Her mouth formed words but no sound came out.

He frowned. "I've spoken too abruptly. I've given you a shock. Forgive me. I meant to lead up to this in a gentler fashion, but there seems no kind way to say what has to be said."

"You . . . you can't mean this, Charles," she burst out.

"I'm afraid I do. I've given the matter a great deal of thought."

"The hell you have!"

"Polly, really."

"You sit there cold-bloodedly talking about age gaps and being sensible. This isn't a contract for building a block of flats, you know. It's my future – our future."

"Please lower your voice," he hissed.

"My voice is at a perfectly reasonable level," she hissed back.

"I must say I didn't expect this rather melodramatic reaction," he said. "I'm most perturbed."

"Perturbed? I doubt it. That would be too strong an emotion for you, Charles." She clapped her hand to her mouth. "I didn't mean that. I don't know what came over me." She felt the floor wobbling under her feet. "Charles," she began again, swallowing her distress, "we were going to talk about our wedding plans tonight. I mean, if you want to put everything on hold for a while, that's okay by me. I don't want to rush you into getting married at Easter. We could make it later in the year."

His gaze slid from hers and a hint of colour came into his cheeks.

"I mentioned another factor. I find this more difficult to say, Polly, because you may think I have been acting in an underhand manner, but that has not been the case, I assure you." He hesitated. There was obviously some inner struggle taking place. She watched in bewilderment as embarrassment and something suspiciously like guilty pleasure showed on his face. "We were rather thrown together by circumstances . . . and you were occupied with your work. You see, she has been such a source of comfort."

"Do you mean there's another woman?"

He looked pained. "I would rather express it less luridly. The mutual attraction we feel has taken us both rather by suprise. One hardly expects in middle age to suddenly be confronted by such a strength of . . . of affection. She is a kind and charming woman with a great many skills and social assets. We are . . . that is, we have grown very close in the short time we have known each other. Last weekend, for example, while you were away she was the most enormous help to me."

"So this affair *has* been going on behind my back! No wonder you had no time to meet me this week."

"It is not an affair. Not in the way you mean. Megan and I—"

"*Megan Lacey!*"

The colour in his cheeks deepened. "I wish to marry her, Polly. That is the truth of it. I'm sorry."

"You've fallen for Megan Lacey." Polly snorted incredulously. "I don't believe it." Then, in an instant, she had a picture of Megan playing the efficient hostess at Charles's party; of Megan, exquisitely groomed, blending perfectly with the tasteful decor of Charles's house. "I do believe it," she said, astonished.

"I didn't want to hurt you," he said regretfully, "but circumstances do change."

"People change, too," she said, staring down at her plate. No longer angry. No longer bewildered. No longer anything much. Just empty, limp.

"Will you make an effort to understand, my dear?" His eyes pleaded with her.

After a moment she nodded. "Yes, Charles," she said miserably. "Yes, I will. I think I do already." Slowly she pulled off her engagement ring and placed it on the table between them.

"Please," he protested, "keep the ring. It's the least you deserve."

"No, Charles," she said. "I think it's best to make a clean break." She managed a tight smile as she rose to her feet. "I'll go home now."

"Please stay. We can still be friends, can't we?"

"I don't know." She honestly didn't.

He made to rise. "I'll run you back."

"I'd rather get a taxi," she said. "Good luck, Charles. I hope you'll both be very happy."

Vee's hairdressing salon was in a quiet back street and already busy when Polly got there at an hour when she was usually lingering over the day's first cup of coffee. A girl with pre-Raphaelite locks and an unceasing flow of chit-chat snipped, rinsed, waved a hairdryer, snipped again, brushed enthusiastically and stood back, exclaiming, "You've got super hair. So easy to manage. But you should look after it better. Have it cut regularly. Like it? Good. My regards to Kate." Then she bounced off to tend another customer.

Polly paid a small fortune at the desk and glanced bemusedly at her reflection in the mirrored walls. Her neck felt cool and bare and her hair had a rich dark-red gloss in the artificial light. But did she like it? She wasn't sure. It seemed so shorn. Neat, though. Bang up to date. She hoped it would impress Mr Moon. That was, after all, the purpose of the exercise.

She walked home slowly, her mind going over and over that scene with Charles last evening. She could still hardly believe that it had happened. That Charles had, in a few brief moments, detached himself from her life. She felt – well, she didn't quite know how she felt. She was in a sort of limbo. There was regret there, and fear, but it was distant, as though everything that had happened had happened to someone else.

Charles had jilted her, turned her world upside down. That was all that she needed to understand.

Perhaps, as Kate had said, she really was a babe in arms when it came to men and relationships. There was only one thing that was solid and real and understandable and that was her work. It was the one area where she was efficient and talented and valued – and that's what she must concentrate on. She'd get through this bad patch purely through her own efforts. And if it meant dressing up and creating a glossy image to impress Mr Moon, then that was what she would damn well do.

If she'd wanted confirmation that the new image was a success she only had to look at Aunt Hester's face when they met.

Her aunt was sitting in a deep uncomfortable-looking chair – chosen, doubtless because it revealed her elegantly slim legs to advantage – in the foyer of her Knightsbridge hotel. She glanced up from the magazine she was flicking through, an interested but detached expression on her face as Polly walked towards her. She could have been observing any stranger – any tall, well-dressed, glossy-haired young woman whose appearance she approved of warmly.

Polly, chin up, eyes ahead, had the uncomfortable sensation that other heads turned as she passed. It was something she hadn't experienced before. She didn't know whether to feel nervous or pleased.

"Polly," her aunt exclaimed. "It can't be! But it is!" The green eyes were wide, the emeralds on her fingers sparkled as her hands lifted in surprise.

"You'd better believe it," Polly said grimly. "And Kate had better be right. This lot" – the gesture took in the hairdo, the grey trousers, the white silk shirt, the loose jacket in shades of grey, tobacco and black, the high-heeled shoes – "cost an arm and a leg."

"Sensational," her aunt breathed. "I never thought to see the day, but 'wow' twice over."

Polly glanced at her watch. "Would you mind if we just grab a cup of coffee? I'll have to cancel lunch, I'm afraid. I'm running late and I've this important client to meet."

She took Hester's arm and steered her into the coffee lounge. A young Italian waiter sprang instantly to their side, lingered rather too long as he took their order and cast an undeniably lustful glance at Polly from melting brown eyes as he departed.

"You see!" her aunt cried triumphantly.

"See what?" Polly asked.

Hester's finely etched eyebrows rose. She shook her head, laughing. "I have to hand it to you,. darling, you haven't an ounce of conceit in your head."

"What I've got in my head doesn't bear close examination," Polly said gloomily. "It's a total mess in there." She lifted her ringless left hand and waved it under her aunt's nose. "Charles has fallen for another woman, the louse. One with iron corsets who knits livers and kidneys for a hobby." She wanted to cover her own sense of failure with banter and jokes, but to her horror she felt tears well up and had to grope for a handkerchief. "Oh heavens, now my mascara will run. Wretched stuff."

Aunt Hester gaped. "Charles has what?"

"You heard. He's jilted me in favour of having his brow mopped by his own personal Flo Nightingale."

"That Lacey woman? Good God."

Polly blew her nose. Hester reached out and touched Polly's arm. "Darling, I'm so sorry. Sorry you've been hurt, that is. But I can't pretend I'm not relieved."

"You never wanted me to marry him."

"True. He wasn't right for you."

"He was," Polly protested. "No one could have been kinder or more generous."

"Or more staid and smug and deadly conventional."

"Just because you didn't get on with him there's no need to be nasty about him. He loved me, I know he did," she wailed. "But he's got this bee in his bonnet about the difference in our ages, and that awful Megan Lacey is just the sort of woman to manipulate everything to her own advantage. We were fine until she came along."

The waiter, who had raced back at lightning speed, was now taking an inordinately long time about pouring out coffee and placing sugar and cream at precise positions on the table, at the same time throwing yearning glances of sympathy at an unheeding Polly.

"I hate to disillusion you," Hester said briskly, "but I've always been convinced that Charles was attracted to you because of sentimental memories of your mother."

"What do you mean, my mother?"

"He was madly in love with her in his formative years. Believe it or not but it's true. She quite spoiled him for anyone else. Then you grew up and he spied a resemblance to his lost love."

Polly's jaw dropped. "But I'm nothing like my mother."

"If you were sitting in my place, darling, looking at you as you are now, you wouldn't say that."

The waiter's thin brown hand paused in the act of shuffling the sugar bowl an inch to the right.

"They were all at university together. You know that much," Hester went on, "and that your father and Charles were boyhood friends. What you don't know is that they were rivals when it came to your mother."

"But I thought Mum and Dad were sweethearts from schooldays."

"They were. But what I've never told you is that Laura

was a terrible flirt." She smiled reminiscently. "It was always John, really, but she wasn't above giving Charles the impression that he had a chance, poor devil. I was still at school, then. I thought it all incredibly romantic. Anyway, once she settled on John, he didn't waste any time. He insisted that they got married straight away. It was what she wanted, too."

Polly swallowed. "My mother . . . what was she like?"

"Beautiful, brilliant, full of life and energy, with that invisible, potent sexual aura that drew men towards her like moths to a flame." Aunt Hester sighed. "Bit of a waste, really. She only had eyes for John. Though, as I say, she'd flirt with any man she was talking to – in the nicest possible way. Oh, I know you'll say it's the pot calling the kettle. I do it all the time. But my brand of flirtation is something I've had to learn. More of a social attribute. With your mother, it was inborn. Part of her make-up and as natural as breathing."

"Didn't my dad mind?"

Hester stirred her coffee thoughtfully. "If he did, he never showed it. He loved her very much. He trusted her. And I think that trust was justified. She would never have deliberately hurt him, she just enjoyed the attention other men gave her. No more than that. They seemed a golden couple to me: lucky in their marriage, a beautiful child, an exciting shared career . . . Then the bubble burst. In the ghastliest possible way." She spread her hands, her green eyes glinting with tears. "Such a terrible waste. I adored her. I miss her still."

The waiter settled the cream jug in its final position, stood back reluctantly and turned his attention to adjusting a pot plant on a nearby table, conveniently within earshot.

"Poor old Charles," Hester went on, after a moment. "He never lost hope that Laura would one day tire of John and their wandering life, and turn to him."

"So sad," Polly whispered.

"He'd probably deny it, but I think your attraction for him all along has been the glimpses he sees in you of Laura."

"But I'm nothing like her."

"So you keep telling me. In temperament, certainly, you're more like your father. He was calm and practically minded. And you have his eyes. But your bone structure, your gestures, the way you talk . . . you're all Laura sometimes."

Polly looked at her, bewildered. "I never realised . . . but she was beautiful. I know I'm not."

"Perhaps not in the same way. But you've the potential to be a striking woman, darling. I've told you so often. I can't tell you how pleased I am that at last you're beginning to make something of yourself."

"My last clear memory of her," Polly said softly, "was of her standing outside that house where it . . . it happened, with the sun on her hair – that red-gold hair – and she was laughing. I was so proud because she was my mother. I wanted to be just like her . . ." Her voice trailed away, then strengthened suddenly. "After that . . . after that terrible time, I didn't want to be like her any more." She stared unseeingly into her coffee cup. "Perhaps, perhaps I felt . . . sensed . . . that evil had somehow been drawn to her, because of her beauty. That frightened me."

Hester shook her head. "It was about tribal vengeance and those men not being given work on the dig."

"I knew that. But still. In a child's mind everything can

become distorted. And perhaps I had picked up signals. Children often understand more than grown-ups give them credit for. I'd seen the way she attracted men . . . and then, what happened . . . at the end . . . somehow it all became mixed-up and twisted about."

Hester reached out and gripped her hand tightly. "Don't think about it, darling. It's over now. You've managed wonderfully to put it all behind you and it's best that way."

"I've never forgotten," she said simply. "I thought I had, but it was there all the time, haunting me, making me afraid. Leon forced me to see that I had to bring it out into the open if I was ever to be rid of the horror."

"Ah, yes, Leon." Her aunt gave her hand a comforting pat and leant back in her chair.

"I know you've talked about me to him. You must have told him something about . . . about what happened."

"A little," said Hester cautiously.

Polly smiled sadly. "He was right. I didn't think so at the time, but it has helped. Everything, now, seems to have lost the sharp, terrifying edge that it had. It's like looking at an old film that's been played so often it's gone blurry at the edges." She sipped her coffee. The bitter aftertaste lay sharp on her tongue. "As for Charles jilting me. Well, after what you've told me, perhaps that's for the best too. At least, it makes it all a bit more understandable."

"Good girl."

Polly laughed. It suddenly seemed extraordinarily funny that Charles should have fallen for Megan Lacey. "You'll have to meet the new fiancée. Boy, will she have him organised."

"Remind me to send them something totally unsuitable for a wedding present."

The waiter beamed and drifted away to attend to an elderly lady who had been signalling frantically for several minutes.

"If that randy young waiter's anything to go by, you'll not be short of male company for long," Hester said, then waved her hand impatiently as Polly looked blank. "Believe me, darling. You're not the plain Jane you've always imagined yourself. And now the butterfly's begun to emerge from the chrysalis, there's no going back."

"If you're talking about this gear I've got on, it's purely an expedient measure. I'm only out to impress this Texan bloke. Mr Moon, would you believe?"

"It's not only the clothes," Hester said. "It's a change of attitude. Already I can see a difference. You're looking a lot more confident."

"How can you say that?"

"Easily. Because it's true."

"But I've just been chucked over by a man who's been part of my life for as long as I can remember," Polly wailed.

"And a good thing too. But I don't think Charles Gregson has much to do with this new Polly I see bursting forth."

"No, it's Kate's fault."

"Really? Nothing to do with Leon Hammond, then?"

Polly stiffened. "Why should it?"

"Oh, from what you were saying, darling, I gathered you were on better terms now."

"No, we're not," she said flatly. "In fact I shan't be working with him any more. I've dropped the assignment."

"What a pity." She gave Polly an enigmatic look. "I had hopes for you there. Such a charming man."

Polly rose to her feet, picked up her bag, dropped a
quick kiss on her aunt's cheek. "Thanks for the coffee
and the chat," she said softly. "It's already helping me to
get everything in perspective. But I'm late, I must fly."

"Fly me to the Moon," Hester warbled.

Polly exited on a groan.

She arrived at the hotel with only minutes to spare. It
had been a tortuous journey through thick traffic. She'd
half wished she'd taken the Tube, but her folder of
work was cumbersome to lug about on public transport.
Besides, while she was driving she was in control. It
was only during the hold-ups that her mind tended to
wander down unsettling blind alleys. She'd expected to be
brooding about Charles but her treacherous subconscious
kept throwing Leon's name, his face, into her thoughts.

She told herself to keep her mind on the job. That had
to be her lifeline, the only reality in a shifting world. She
was a good photographer with a sound reputation. She was
going to turn herself into the best. To blazes with men and
a life fraught with emotional upset!

This resolution carried her into the lobby of the hotel.
She felt cool, in command, pleasurably anticipating the
meeting as she wove through a press of people and
mounds of luggage. Must be a delayed plane, there was
such a crowd. Waiting her turn at the reception desk, she
became aware of tension in the air. One receptionist was
trying to calm a woman who seemed likely to be overtaken
by hysterics.

"Sorry to keep you waiting," the receptionist apologised
when she eventually turned her attention to Polly. "Miss
Burton for Mr Moon. Oh, yes." She smiled brightly.
"Unfortunately he had to leave the hotel earlier than

anticipated. He left this for you." She produced an envelope. "He asked me to give you his sincere regrets for altering the arrangements."

Polly tore open the envelope. A brief typed note explained that if she could get over to Terminal 1 within the hour and have him paged, he'd be pleased to talk to her. She could. Mr Moon was important. She wasn't going to let him out of the country that easily.

"Thanks," she said. "And if Mr Moon contacts you, tell him I'm on my way."

The overwrought woman nearby burst into noisy sobs.

"Poor woman," the receptionist confided. "The emergency number's engaged and she can't get news of her husband. It's the hotel fire – the one in Jersey," she explained. "Haven't you heard? It's been on all the news bulletins this morning. Some sort of gas explosion they believe – people missing and injured. Her husband had just arrived there for a conference, apparently."

"Conference?" Polly's heart suddenly missed a beat. The envelope crumpled in her fingers. "What conference?" she demanded loudly, as the receptionist turned to the next guest.

"The big international wildlife one," the girl said, flinging over her shoulder the last bit of ghastly information. "The hotel was reserved for the delegates."

Polly stood as if turned to stone. She felt like she'd been dealt an enormous, breath-stopping blow to her midriff. *Leon*! Her mind screamed his name. *Leon*! She saw smoke and flame and confusion. She saw him crumpled amid burning debris, borne on a shrouded stretcher, trapped on some teetering upper floor.

She took an instinctive step towards the telephone. There was an emergency number. Engaged, the girl had said. Vaguely, she noted that the distraught woman was being led away. Around her, strangers lugged cases, flowed in and out of the lobby. There was still a tense knot of people at the desk. She wanted to push them aside, grab the phone, shout his name to whoever would listen, demand to know if he was alive.

Her hand flew to her throat where a pulse beat fast and hard. She mustn't panic. She must think, plan, act sensibly.

Mr Moon's letter was crumpled in her hand. She focussed on it slowly. She still had an appointment. Once she got to the terminal surely she'd be able to get more information? And Mr Moon, maybe he could help. If he was rich and influential, he'd perhaps be able to find out more than she could.

She ran, suddenly galvanised, out of the hotel. And if, she thought wildly, anything had happened to Leon, she would get the next plane out to Jersey. What could be easier? She was on the spot.

She didn't remember afterwards anything of the drive to the airport. She didn't remember parking the car or running into the terminal. She was racked with fear and despair, saying over and over again, "Please let Leon be safe. I let him go out of my life. He never knew how I truly felt about him. I can't bear it if I never see him again."

More crowds . . . queues of people, rows of luggage trolleys . . . a blur of noise. She found an enquiries desk. Could scarcely remember the reason for being there. Made an effort to pull herself together, to speak clearly.

"Mr Moon," she said. "I have to meet him. There should be some sort of a message . . . or he has to be paged . . . Oh, blow him. Please . . . I can't think straight. This fire in Jersey. I know somebody who should be at the hotel.

I'm desperate to know about him, if he's all right. Do you know anything about it?"

"I'm so sorry." The girl looked sympathetic. "Will you wait one moment and I'll see what I can find out. And I do have a message for you, if you're Miss Burton. Mr Moon left this."

Another envelope, bulkier this time. Had she missed him again? Was this the brush-off? She didn't really care. But it was important to keep her hands occupied while the girl was on the phone.

She slid her nail under the flap. Some sort of a booklet. No, a ticket. The corner of her mind that wasn't occupied with Leon noted that it was an airline ticket. There was a note attached. She opened it. Not typewritten this one, but printed in bold, handwritten capital letters.

She read it twice before it made sense.

'POLLY BURTON, I NEED YOU TO PHOTO-GRAPH MY HOUSE, MY ANIMALS, MY CRUMB-LING WELSH RUIN. I PROMISE TO LOVE YOU AND YOUR CAMERA TILL DEATH US DO PART, IF YOU'LL RUN AWAY TO JERSEY WITH ME THIS VERY MINUTE. WILL YOU MARRY ME POLLY? I'VE A SPECIAL LICENCE IF YOU'RE WILLING TO TAKE THE CHANCE. MAHLEN D. MOON II'

A hand touched her shoulder. She spun round. She looked up into a pair of deep-blue eyes. She felt her bones melting away to water.

She didn't think. She was past thinking. She just flung herself into his arms, her hands tightening in the dark, rough hair on the nape of his neck. His grip almost knocked the breath from her body, but she didn't care. His voice was in her ear, his hands crushed her ribs, his warm mouth traced little light kisses over her cheek.

"Polly," he whispered. "Oh, Polly, sweetheart. Does this mean what I hope it means?"

"I thought you were injured. Or worse! The fire in Jersey. I nearly went out of my mind!"

Behind them the girl at the desk cleared her throat. Reluctantly they released each other, returning to the world of noise and bustle, and to the smiling glances of passers-by.

The girl beamed. "I've made enquiries, Miss Burton. You'll be glad to know that the situation is not as serious as was thought at first. Most people seem to have got out safely. A few people have minor injuries, but the fire is under control and there's been much less damage than was first thought."

"Fire?" Leon said, frowning. "What's all this?"

"Later," Polly said, and frowned at him. "You owe more than you know to it. It brought me to my senses. More to the point, why aren't you in Jersey? and what's all this about Mahlen D. Moon?"

Leon grinned. "The well-known anagram."

Polly looked at him blankly. Then, "Leon Hammond. Of course. You double-dealing, cheating, lying—"

"Cut the flattery, my darling," he said, laughing. "And I'm not due to speak at the conference until tomorrow." He slipped an arm round her shoulders and began to lead her through the crowds. "We have an hour to spare before the plane goes."

She stopped dead in her tracks. "I haven't said I'm going yet. Besides I haven't any luggage."

"You have," he said. "I took the liberty of ordering a

The Glass Case

few indecent garments, including a replica of the one I gave you at Christmas. I still think you'll look amazing in it."

"But how? Why?" she began. "Last time we spoke you hung up on me." She shuddered at the recollection.

"You have a clever girl called Kate who works for you."

"Kate! Was she in on this charade?"

"She sent me an invoice for services rendered with, 'She's eating her heart out' written across it in purple ink."

"Treachery! I'm surrounded by traitors."

"You're surrounded by people who love you and want you to be happy." He hugged her. "People like me."

"And what about Charles?" she said. "Not given much thought to him, have you?"

"The end justifies the means," he said, looking a touch shamefaced.

She glanced at him mischievously. She thought she'd wait a little while before she told him that she was actually a spurned woman. Give him a taste of his own medicine. Mahlen D. Moon, indeed.

He kissed the tip of her nose. She smiled up at him. "I'm so lucky. I thought I'd lost you."

"Not afraid any more? Are you ready to take a chance on love?"

She tested the thought carefully.

"I know I want to be with you. I can't bear the thought that you'd get on the plane and leave me behind. Is that enough for now?"

"The glass case?"

"In a million splinters," she said. And smiled.